IT WAS A CHOICE OF EVILS . . .

It was one thing to come out of the sanctuary of the ship, peel down the soft bark layers of a woodplant, saw the harder xylem beneath into planks and beams which could be dried stiffly into place and form shelter. But risking the delicate balance of their bodies was a very different matter.

It would be intolerable to see the vigor and enthusiasm of the colonists drained away by the insidious leech of scurvy. But at the edge of his mind the shadow lurked, which was Death. He was sure that Earthly plants grown in Asgard soil contained a substance which would negate the impact of the local bacterium on the human metabolism. So far none of the control animals fed on locally grown plants had shown signs of disease, but a man was not a pig or a rat.

He said harshly, "I think we shall have to call for volunteers!"

Also by John Brunner
Published by Ballantine Books:

DOUBLE, DOUBLE

THE INFINITIVE OF GO

THE LONG RESULT

PLAYERS AT THE GAME OF PEOPLE

THE SHEEP LOOK UP

SHOCKWAVE RIDER

STAND ON ZANZIBAR

THE WHOLE MAN

CATCH A FALLING STAR

BEDLAM PLANET

JOHN BRUNNER

A Del Rey Book

BALLANTINE BOOKS • NEW YORK

A Del Rey Book
Published by Ballantine Books

Author's Note:

In writing this novel I have made extensive use of the
Larousse Encyclopedia of Mythology (the English version
of *Larousse Mythologie Generale*) and am in consequence
indebted to its compilers, editors and translators.

Copyright © 1968 by Brunner Fact and Fiction, Ltd.

ISBN 0-345-30678-3

Manufactured in the United States of America

First Ballantine Books Edition: November 1982

Cover art by Darrell K. Sweet

ONE THE NAKED MAN

From the hag and hungry goblin
That into rags would rend ye
And the spirit that stands by the naked man
In the Book of Moons defend ye!
That of your five sound senses
You never be forsaken
Nor travel from yourselves with Tom
Abroad to beg your bacon.

    Nor never sing, "Any food, any feeding,
    Money, drink or clothing?
    Come dame or maid, be not afraid—
    Poor Tom will injure nothing."

—Tom o' Bedlam's Song

I

DREAMING . . .

Assailed by the presence of the gashed terrible reproving moon in the hysterical silence of the night Dennis Malone lay on his bed and writhed without waking, his spasms wasted because they could not break his shackles of exhaustion.

Set up on a monstrous peak towering infinite light-years above the bottomless abyss, he was the target in a cockshy where the balls came thick as hailstones, moon-huge, each gashed with that accusing mouth eloquent of disaster, and sometimes the mouth opened in the face of an avenging Jehovah, uttering curses upon him and all his seed.

Interstellar distances are God's quarantine regulations.

At last anguish thrust down from the violent activity of his cortex and made his whole spine a long shaft of pain. He jerked into awareness like a frog spiked with a hot poker. His eyelids snapped up and stayed pressed by muscular spasm at the limits of his orbits. To exclude the light of the moon he had fastened the door tightly and the shutter over the unglazed window. Some light, though, crept through the ventilation slots under the eaves, and his mad-hungry gaze secured glimpses of form, the outline of familiar furniture. But they were distant from him across a pool of total dark, the floor, and he might as well have been drifting in space where men are robbed of perspective by vacancy. He stifled a moan. Relying on the contact of his skin and his mattress, he gained sufficient control to swing his legs to the floor and tried not to realise that the smooth planks on

3

which he placed his soles had been peeled from the layered bulk of a thing more like a vegetable carbuncle than an honest upright tree. It was wood . . . of a sort.

The shudders of horror which he had carried with him from nightmare subsided, little by little. His breathing eased, and the pounding of his heart. It was no good trying to switch on a light—to conserve their irreplaceable generators, power was withdrawn at midnight. He would have to make the voyage across the room to undo the shutter catch. Whereupon he would see—

Stop it!

He trembled again, but this time, he noted with relief, it was a shiver and not a shudder. He had lain down naked as usual, but since he retired the night had called a cool breeze off the sea. By touch he located the suit he had worn the day before and wriggled into it, then walked his toes like insects into the shelter of the shoes he would rather have gone without but which against the risk of as yet undiscovered parasites or infection were enjoined on everyone. If there were a creature like a chigger, for example, which could bore up through even the toughest skin of a human heel . . .

Am I sick?

He knew the answer to the question was affirmative even as he put it to himself, but he made no move towards the self-diagnosing medikit with which he and everyone else in the village was equipped. He had a contagious disease, certainly, which was why he slept alone, and it consisted in aloneness, and it could not be cured by company. He must sweat it out like a fever for which there was no specific, and he might for all his struggles fail to conquer.

Deliberately, like a suicide, he took the four long steps to the window, fumbled with the shutter catch, and drew back the frame of boards that blocked out the night. Beyond, the sky was black and deep as cat's fur, speckled with stars like drops of fine rain. He felt his head rise and turn, seemingly in response to a programme, not a decision, and saw the damaged moon sliding towards the horizon.

It was just a chunk of barren rock, like Earth's moon, with a straight slash across the lower part of its oblate disc.

Vaguely surprised that his subconscious had not instantly re-created the nightmare image and made it come hurtling at him like a hunting missile, he waited until he was sure it was stable. Then, because even now he dared not return to sleep where fresh horrors might ambush him, he made for the door and went out into the wrongly scented night.

Everyone else seemed to be enjoying peaceful slumber. He felt a stab of resentment, but knew the reason: their exhaustion, though as great as his, could be tempered by satisfaction. And they had good cause for it. They had a village to live in, with a street—or at least a winding track, surfaced with compacted broken shells, heat-fused, then roughened to a texture right for walking on a rainy day. From the inland peak on which the *Santa Maria* rested like the egg of a roc, down to the natural harbour where small boats were secured among jutting boulders, it made two curves and formed an S. Along it were disposed buildings that provided evidence—slim, but precious—of humanity. Nothing else here, that they had discovered, had conceived the straight line or the level plane surface.

Under dogmatically right-angled eaves, enclosed by shingles and planks they had cut themselves, his companions slept in peace. They had what they wanted. Whereas he, Dennis Malone . . .

His feet were carrying him in the usual direction, towards the spot where he had experienced that mad fit of lust and risked the loss of his life, the destruction of a billion hopes, on the gratification of a passing impulse. He went back to it again and again, as though some eventual visit would furnish him with explanations for it. The deed had been so foreign to his normal self-control that it was impossible to categorise in memory except by stuffing it into a grab-bag of other unique associations whose only common link was "being on another planet."

Would it help to have Sigrid here, who at first had been rational while he was frenzied, so that he came close to raping her, then finally gave way as though swept along with him in a torrent of psychic need that made the anticipation of death negligible?

But she could not be here. She was on Earth. And if she could miraculously be transported to stand before him, it would be a meaningless event.

What armour do I wear against reason? We calculate, we analyse, we deduce, and think we have planned for all eventualities. But what impulses lurk below the surface of the mind, which never could be allowed for in advance because it took the impact of an alien planet to trigger them?

He turned aside from the track which he had been automatically following, and clambered up a slope carpeted with the juicy, moss-like growths which filled the ecological niche occupied on Earth by grasses. At the top of the rise he sat down on a convenient woodplant. To grow beyond a certain minimum size, to sustain its respiration which helped to keep the air oxygen-high, this and all related species had adopted the same solution to the problem of surface versus volume as the human brain; it was convoluted like a walnut. By day it looked rather repulsive. But the outer, bark-like layers were soft and made a good resting-place. Only the deeper tissues were hard and woody.

From here he had a clear view of the small natural harbour, the roofs of the village, the looming globe of the ship. To distract himself from that other globe, the moon, he began to employ the hard facts which one day would become the material of a historical record for the schoolchildren of the city which must succeed their new-built village.

If we survive . . .

But he blocked that out with verbalisations, treating the air as though it were a rather dull primary pupil in a distant generation.

"When they deciphered the reports of the first robot probe to return from Sigma Draconis—one of a fleet of hundreds which had been launched through the curious not-here-ness of qua-space towards nearby stars that astronomers held to be promising—the scientists of Earth were inclined to suspect malfunction in the recorders that had stored the information, even though Sigma Draconis was rather like Sol. After the disappointments of Tau Ceti, Alpha Centauri, Epsilon Eridani and other systems whose primaries had proved to mother mere barren balls of rock and gas, it was incredible to learn of a planet close in size to Earth, warmer so that its icecaps were seasonal and its oceans deeper, yet equally endowed with taller crustal deformities so that its surface was webbed with archipelagoes, the summits of submarine mountains, and possessing moreover a large, nearly Luna-sized, satellite whose tides had encouraged life to emerge from the sea and colonise the land.

"When they had been convinced by the agreement between the data gathered by the first probe, and those from the second and third, they converted one of the probes to carry four curious persons, poised at that improbable fulcrum of awareness where explorers live. Because they had to be enclosed together for nearly four years first in a fragile cockleshell of a starship, then on a world unseen by human eyes, and then in the ship again, they were all in a sense lovers. But what sustained them was the shared discovery of a greater hunger: the lust for knowledge.

"They called the ship the *Argo*. If that matters. And the world they called Asgard, the place in heaven reached across Bifrost, the rainbow bridge.

"In order of setting foot on the planet's surface, the first visitors were Dennis Malone, Carmen Vlady, Pyotr Tang-Lin and Sigrid Kallela. They lived for five months on Asgard, deliberately—"

And once without intention. But one would not wish to burden a school-child with the problem which had caused Earth's leading psychologists to peel down his personality like an onion, to the final weak green core, in search of the explanation for it, before conceding ultimately that it might have stemmed from a need to impose the most basic element of human experience on a totally new environment, and agreeing that by a miracle it had done no harm. So:

"Deliberately exposing themselves to the new planet to determine its habitability. When they brought home a favourable report, an expedition was mounted which consisted of three ships named the *Pinta,* the *Niña* and the *Santa Maria* (after the ocean-going vessels of the expedition led by Christopher Columbus, *q.v.* under 'Terrestrial History'), crewed by volunteers who planned to colonise the newly discovered world.

"Unfortunately, in those pioneering days, the control which could be exercised over the resultant velocity at which a ship emerged from qua-space was rudimentary. When the *Pinta* returned to our normal universe, she was on a course which led to a grazing collision with Asgard's satellite. Among those killed was Pyotr Tang-Lin, one of the two members of the original expedition who had agreed to act as guides for the colonists."

He stared upward, across three hundred thousand miles, and wondered for a moment how the moon had looked before the *Pinta* had died there in thirty seconds of hell, like the passage of a match-head across sandpaper. Alarmed, he discovered that he could not remember. The first time, he had not been looking at the moon through the eyes of a child eager to make patterns of the dark maria.

But if only they hadn't combined to suggest two eyes, a skull-pit nose, brows arching up across a hydrocephalic idiot's forehead, to which the new formation added the last touch: a lop-sided mouth set in a permanent mocking leer.

He had been up there. He had touched, albeit through gauntlets, the rough-and-smooth surface of fused rock, seen the bright gobbets of spattered metal, steel-white, gold-yellow, cobalt-blue, embedded like shrapnel in the bones of the satellite. There was no one who could be held to blame for what had happened. It was blind chance.

And now here he was, on warm hospitable Asgard, where each breath he drew should remind him of the welcome the alien visitors had received: comfortable, well-nourished, healthy because there were so few native organisms which found human tissue congenial for infection. It was no use. In the silent cavern of his skull he cried the truth.

I didn't want to be made welcome! I wanted to go home!

But he spoke aloud again, levelly, still picturing that unknown child a century hence, and said, "Although there could not be any more starships built in the immediate future, since producing them had strained even the incredible resources of modern Earth and no more were planned unless a still more promising planet should be discovered—which was unlikely—the loss of the *Pinta* was not an irremediable calamity except to one member of the expedition. Although with the wreck had gone many of the key experts, especially biologists, and many important supplies including computer-memories, the survival of the colony had not been made dependent on having all three ships available. It had been intended that one should be cannibalised, broken down into millions of valuable parts from the enormous fusion-generators which had supplied the power to blast her into qua-space clear through to the plainest sheet-metal bulkhead capable of being stamped into fence-nails; one should remain intact on the planet in case total evacuation should become necessary in emergency; and one should return to Earth after a year, piloted by Pyotr Tang-Lin and the other second-time visitor, Dennis Malone, taking along any of the colonists who had been overcome by uncontrollable nostalgia, or proved subject to an incurable allergy, or in some other way unsuitable to remain on Asgard.

"After half that time had passed, there were as yet no signs that any colonists would need to return. They had been screened and screened again, until those who were chosen were identified beyond doubt as settlers, capable of uprooting and re-planting themselves. There was only one person on the whole new world for whom the *Pinta*'s loss might truly be called disastrous, and it was so to him because he was not a settler. He was an explorer. And he wished, and wished, and *wished* it might have been himself and not Pyotr who died on the alien moon."

He gazed up, eyes aching, fists clenched so that his nails drove deep into his palms. It occurred to him to wonder when that satellite had ceased to be Sigma Draconis III/1 and become simply "the moon", because he felt vaguely that the change was in some way significant, but he was incapable of following the thought to a conclusion. He could only sit stiller than a rock and stare at it, and suffer.

II

TALL, SLIM, GRACEFUL, golden-brown, her sleek black hair grown out now to nape-length since she had left the ship where long tresses might prove dangerous in the event of air-loss and the need to seal spacegear within seconds, Parvati Chandra sat at Abdul Hassan's table in the administrative office and sifted through the summary reports which all the specialist departments had forwarded for consideration at today's progress meeting. It was another hot day; in the corner of the room, a primitive mechanical fan struggled to stir the sluggish air which seeped through the open window.

But she had been used to a warm humid climate most of her life, at home on Earth. The weather didn't distract her. She had paid it as much attention as she meant to today, while she was reading Kitty Minakis's report on the probable pattern of the climate during the fall.

Satisfied that the report contained nothing alarming, she had put it aside, taking up in its place that from Ulla Berzelius regarding materials and resources. Despite her almost inhuman power of detachment—compelled on her by the need to watch every movement and practically every though of the colonists with more than paranoid suspicion—she felt a stir of excitement as she scanned the sheets. Last month Ulla had gloomily concentrated on the possibility of re-designing their planned equipment in terms of the aluminium and silica which could be got merely by shoveling up beach-sand. Now, here she was talking about gallium, indium, germanium; about a rock analogous to pitchblende with a high radioactive count; about a native form of fluorspar from which they could extract fluorine and, if required, employ the ancient process of gaseous diffusion to make fuel for a fission pile.

Parvati made a check-mark on the margin of the copy of the schedule which lay before her, detailing the predicted stages of the conquest of Asgard. This island where the settlers had landed had been chosen by the original team of four explorers as ideal for a first colony. It was neither small nor large—extensive enough to offer plenty of data by which they could judge the true habitability of Asgard, yet not so big that its unexplored recesses might hide serious threats like carnivores or poisonous plants to kill over-confident and ignorant children when they started their families. It was steep enough to resist the tides. It was located in a temperate climatic zone where the fauna of the ocean were neither as fierce as in the equatorial waters nor as frenzied as at the poles, where the annual melting of the ice poured incredible volumes of nutriment into the sea and provoked a fantastic outburst of ravening greed.

Nonetheless, in spite of all these advantages, the programme for the settlement had been laid out in gradual stages. By policy, to impress beyond doubt on the colonists that this was *not* tame, domesticated Earth, they had gone straight to grips with their new home. Instead of retreating nightly to the security of durasteel bulkheads, they cut native wood and fashioned huts like barracks, partitioned to afford privacy to those who had paired off, or who preferred to sleep alone. They made furniture. Currently they were baking pots of clay, since a suitable deposit had been found near the inland peak where the *Santa Maria* rested. It was no use relying on something manufactured lightyears away by the peak tools of terrestrial technology, when without warning they might be left naked and desperate.

And yet . . .

Parvati hesitated. At last she nodded and shrugged, and decided the gamble was justifiable. She was going to recommend to Hassan, at the progress meeting, that they omit some of the slow stages from their schedule. They could scarcely expect to leap ahead to programmed dwellings, polysensory entertainment channels and all the other trappings of the leisured culture they had left, not within the lifetimes of the first arrivals. But at the back of her mind she had always nursed the vague hope that here, with a chance to start over, mankind might avoid some of the worst mistakes he had committed at home: raping fertile lands until they became dustbowls, hunting animals like whales until it was too late to prevent their extinction, squandering irreplaceable coal and oil in furnaces and cars when they would eventually be needed as a source of food.

It looked as though that was going to be possible. For instance, according to the report which Hassan himself had prepared—as well as being their chairman and senior administrator, he was their quartermaster and responsible for the use they made of the stores they had brought from Earth, including the surviving ships—their solar collectors were already providing nearly all their power requirements, and if the tidal generators could be installed before winter they could cocoon their fusion generators for emergency use only. That was crucial; refining heavy hydrogen was not on the schedule for another year and a half.

From this starting-point, optimistic conclusions radiated. They could scrap the idea of heating their new home in winter by means of a clay-pipe hot-water system connected to a common boiler, and concentrate the labour freed thereby on producing proper window-glass, a task which had posed unexpected difficulties. Small individual heaters containing unrefined molten salts and plugged into the common power-cable would be far more convenient. And so on.

A shadow crossed the window, and she glanced around. Her brow clouded suddenly as she remembered what she, of all people, ought not to have forgotten for an instant: that it was on their human resources, not the material ones, that their success ultimately depended. She leaned back in her chair, bracing herself. Clearly Dennis Malone was going to come knocking at the door.

In answer to his diffident tap, she called for him to enter, and he stood on the threshold with a look of faint surprise at seeing her rather than Hassan.

"Ah—morning, Parvati," he muttered. "Is Abdul around?"

"He's doing a tour of the island. We have a progress meeting today. Can I help you?"

"Oh yes, of course. I'd forgotten." Dennis seemed distracted, so that his eyes did not meet hers, and she surveyed him covertly while waiting for him to explain his business. She was alarmed at what she saw. His lids were puffy, most likely with lack of sleep, and there were deep lines seaming his forehead. His hands moved together nervously, as though possessed of independent life.

Poor devil!

Briskly, she said, "Well, I'm glad you're here, anyway. I was just thinking yesterday I'd like to give you another checkup. Could you—?"

"Oh, shut up, Parvati," he said. There was no force behind the words. "What could another bunch of tests tell me that you don't know already—that I don't know still better because I'm on the inside? I'm a mess. I'm a wreck. About the only thing we can hope for is that I'll sweat out my problem before it starts to bother anyone else."

"You're exaggerating, Dennis."

"The hell I am." He kicked around a chair, formed bentwood-fashion from slivers of the native woodplant, and slumped into it. "My trouble is that I'm a settler against my will, and not even the colony voting to give me the *Niña* to go home in would cure me, because I'd go crazy during the trip to Earth for fear sacrificing their spare ship meant the colonists were exterminated by something we haven't come across and which they couldn't run away from. Right? Don't bother to answer. I just came in to tell Abdul that I need to go off by myself again."

"So soon? But you only came back from your last trip—"

"It's been two weeks, hasn't it? If I'd picked up any diseases or anything, they'd have shown by now. And what other use can you make of me except send me off to scout the neighbourhood? After all, I'm the only expendable person here."

"A hundred and eighty people on a planet the size of Earth give or take a few per cent, and you think even one of them can be called expendable? Dennis, you're not developing a martyr complex, are you?"

"If I were, you'd have found it out from your tests," Dennis muttered. "Quit fencing with me, Parvati. I *know* that in spite of everything—two hands, strong back, adequate intelligence, technical skills—I'm a liability. Everybody else wanted to be here, everybody else was prepared consciously and subconsciously for the idea of remaining here till their dying day. I'm the only one who's trapped. And it follows from that that I'm the likeliest to go crazy. Something which even you couldn't predict with your fantastic empathy might break me apart one day—a last-straw frustration, more than likely—and you might well lose someone you genuinely can't afford to do without. Isn't that true? Tell me honestly."

But before she had a chance to frame her answer, he rose and headed for the door. "I'll wander round and see who wants some data harvested. Maybe I can come back this afternoon with enough requests to save Abdul from being as obstructionist as you."

The door closed behind him. It was of unseasoned timber. It had been accurately cut with power-tools when it was installed, but it was warping a little now, and when it met its jamb a bulge in the wood rubbed, and caused a squeak. Parvati winced.

Of course, he was perfectly right. Regardless of how well their plan to establish themselves was progressing, they had in the final analysis come naked to Asgard. They had to clothe themselves—indeed, to armour themselves—by power of reason alone. And human beings were not wholly rational creatures.

That imponderable had been taken into account as much as possible, and even there luck had in most ways been on their side. Just as by policy they had set to immediately after arriving to work the native materials by hand, for the sake of the continuing psychological reinforcement which would stem from looking at the street, the houses, the boats and remembering that this was part of Asgard made over by the will of man, so too they had stocked their minds not only with the skills of Earth, but its varied culture and traditions: legend, folklore, literature, everything which could offer a pipeline to the past they had left lightyears behind them.

In a sense which was so cynical that she had not dared discuss it with anyone else, she was even coming to think that the loss of the *Pinta* had been a blessing in disguise. When irrational regret at something not being available on Asgard, though commonplace on Earth, threatened to overwhelm someone, there was a rational ground for resentment to which it might be attached: the fact that instead of the three ships they had expected, there were only two. The crash had laid a long shadow of sorrow across their lives, naturally—every member of the expedition had counted all the others as friends. But, like a wound which healed to a scar without imposing a permanent handicap, that would fade.

The sponsors of the venture had planned well. The lack of the *Pinta* had caused only difficulties, not failure, and perhaps the added incentive had driven people harder than they might have managed without the knowledge that catastrophe really could overtake them. That was just as well. She hated to think what another major setback would do to Hassan. As well as being the senior among them, at fifty, he was a sort of father-figure—deliberately chosen—and looked on the colonists as his family. The loss of the *Pinta* had put him in the predicament of an Abraham who had not escaped the charge to sacrifice his son, and, lacking visible compensation for his deed, he would have crumbled.

Yet he, and she herself, and all the other key members of the colony, were enduring what had to be endured, and gaining strength.

Except Dennis Malone.

With an effort, because she knew he was correct to say his sickness could not be cured unless it were by time and his own self-mastery, she returned to her study of the progress reports. Now, however, the elation had gone from her, and indeed the light seemed to have gone from the bright summer day.

III

AT THE MOMENT the village street was empty, though there were several people in sight on the hillside and along the beach. Everyone had dispersed, after their communal breakfast in the mess-hall, to their daily work. During the first month or so after landing, superfluous Dennis had been in continual demand, called on by all the work-teams whenever a spare pair of hands was needed. Now, things were so well under control he had to go out and beg for assignments.

He walked towards the harbour, more or less at random, his gun bumping his thigh as he went. To be seen without it, or without the medikit which occupied the corresponding pocket on the other side of his suit, would have been to invite the censure and rebuke of all the colonists. Not that he had to be compelled. Everything about his surroundings made him nervous. Even in the womb-like dark of his room at night, there was still the indefinably wrong smell of Asgard to remind him.

On a kind of natural wharf, formed by a slab of rock akin to slate, which ran beside the sandy bay, he found Daniel Sakky, their construction engineer in chief, discussing with shipwright Saul Carpender the siting of the boatsheds that would make their harbour storm-proof for the winter. Daniel was a big jovial African who personalised his standard suit with whatever touches he could find; today, he had given himself a brooch of little spiky egg-cases such as were found washed up on all the nearby beaches, glistening like opals, fastened into an eight-pointed star.

He greeted Dennis cordially, but in response to his

diffident request for something useful he could go looking for, merely shrugged.

"This planet's being too kind to us, Dennis!" he exclaimed. "What I needed was mainly cement and a supply of steel bar, or else a source of structural plastics which could be cured on site. Ulla has found me both, when I could have made do with either. But if I think of anything . . ."

On a rocky promontory further around the island he encountered Kitty Minakis, the tiny fragile Greek meteorologist whom no one would have suspected of being on speaking terms with storms, being helped by an assistant to fill the day's batch of upper-air radiosondes from a small automatic electrolyser that broke up water and supplied the necessary hydrogen. She gave him a flashing smile and contrived to draw down the zip of her suit—already low as though the heat of the day were oppressing her—another inch on her small but beautiful bosom. No one held her fondness for men against her; it was impossible to dislike such a sweet-natured person.

But there was nothing she could suggest for him to do which would furnish the excuse for another scouting trip away from the island. They had left robot weather satellites in orbit as they came down, and all of them were functioning; they had sown surface observation units on equally spaced islands from pole to pole, and they too were signalling on schedule.

He exchanged greetings with a couple of Daniel's staff who were stringing additional power-cables from the solar collectors that had started to fledge the slopes of the island like weird technological shrubs, and came to the stream which they had dammed to provide their fresh water. Ulla Berzelius, her long blonde hair clipped back from her face with a metal comb, was sifting the mud of the exposed bed and picking out small pebbles to put in a box. Beside her, Yoko Namura was lifting, examining, recording with an automatic camera and throwing away the corpses of the little water-creatures which the artificial drought had killed.

"You've done too good a job on your previous trips," Ulla said in answer to his question. "We've located all the minerals which are indispensable already. Right now I'm just looking for indium—our seawater analysers came up with a minute trace which was probably washed out by a stream, and I want to know if it was this stream. But if you like I'll cheerfully tell Abdul a white lie. Even negative knowledge is useful, after all."

She snapped her fingers. "Just a second, though! One thing we don't have, which it would be nice to find in a natural deposit instead of having to make them, and that's diamonds. I'll bet that Abdul would love to have a supply. He keeps asking me hopefully whether the stuff I've located is in hard or soft strata, because we're not overloaded with rock-drill bits. Shall I see if I can work out a list of likely localities for you?"

"Just tell me what to programme the computers for, and I'll do it myself," Dennis said, cheering up instantly. "Blue clay in a young volcanic region—isn't that right?"

Ulla chuckled. "Start concentrating on that, on a world with vigorous tectonics like this one, and you could spend half a lifetime on the job."

"That would be great," Dennis muttered. Not catching his meaning, she gave him a blank look and continued.

"You might as well have a shot at it, though. I think I should have put enough data into the store by now to produce a manageable printout. Just punch for bort—industrial-grade stones. We certainly haven't mapped enough of the local geology to pin down gemstones with any precision."

"Thanks," Dennis said. "Anything I can do for you, Yoko?" he added to the xenobiologist.

"The usual." Yoko shrugged. "Shots of any creature or plant you don't recognise, and enough clues to lead us back to where you spotted it."

"Will do," Dennis said, and climbed back out of the streambed.

The island was roughly hexagonal, with rocky ridges connecting the central peak where the *Santa Maria* rested to each of the promontories. The shallow valleys between the ridges were cluttered with vegetation, except where Tai Men's team had cleared the ground to plant vegetables from Earth in the rich soil there exposed, but on the ridges themselves there were only the warty excrescences of the woodplants. He made his way to the spine of the nearest and started to follow it towards the ship. As he went higher, he was able to see over the island's shoulder, towards the spot where the *Niña* was being systematically dismembered for the sake of its components. The star-brilliance of a cutting torch hurt his eyes as it moved across the gleaming plates of her upper hull, not because it could truly be so bright at this distance, but because at every pass it eroded another of the strands that tied him to Earth, as though he were hanging at the brink of a precipice feeling the stems of a grass-clump break one by one with his weight, and could not tell how few there must be before he fell.

Also he could see the heavily wired pens where their handful of test animals were kept, the survivors which a cautious planner had assigned to *Santa Maria* instead of the *Pinta*. There were plenty of rats and mice thanks to their rapid breeding, but the more useful hamsters and pigs were alarmingly few when one considered how soon human beings must start to eat soil-grown instead of hydroponic food.

However, he was no longer in the mood for gloomy thoughts. Ulla had given him the excuse for an excursion by himself, and that was all he cared about right now. He hastened his steps, remembering that when he first made an ascent like this, in company with Carmen Vlady, the exertion tired him owing to Asgard's eight per cent greater gravity. Now he was used to it and didn't notice. Perhaps, in time, the other strangenesses of the planet would cease to trouble him.

Suddenly, however, he checked. As usual, Tai Men was taking sick call at the entrance to the *Santa Maria*'s main lock, attended by his deputies. He had never seen so many people waiting to be dealt with. There must be a couple of dozen at the least, standing and sitting around, looking worried.

Wondering what could have caused it, yet not wanting to interrupt the medics by inquiring, he made to go straight inship. But, catching sight of him, Tai Men called out.

"Hey, Dennis! Here a moment!"

Complying, he approached the electronic desk with its load of computer remotes, through which the doctors could consult the store of medical knowledge in the memory banks of the ship.

"You feeling all right?" Tai Men demanded. He was above average height for a Chinese, but thanks to his blocky build he gave the impression of squatness—by implication, power and determination. But Dennis had never seen him wear such a grim expression before.

Now very disturbed, he answered truthfully: apart from inadequate sleep, he was well.

"Open your mouth," Tai Men snapped, and peered inside. "Gums been sore at all? Any bleeding?"

"No, none," Dennis said, paling as he made the assumption any spaceman might have reached. "Not checking on overdoses of radiation, are you, Tai?"

"Radiation hell," the biologist in chief said curtly. "*That's* a stupid question, if you like. Here, have one of these." He seized a jar from the table and shook out a large white capsule. By the look of it, he had given one to everybody else here assembled, and the level of the remainder was down to half.

"What is it?" Dennis said, taking the capsule.

"Ascorbic acid. We have twenty-two advanced cases of scurvy, and I can't for the life of me figure out why."

TWO THE LORDLY LOFTS

Of thirty bare years have I
Twice twenty been enragéd
And of forty been three times fifteen
In durance soundly cagéd
In the lordly lofts of Bedlam
On stubble soft and dainty,
Brave bracelets strong, sweet whips ding-dong,
With wholesome hunger plenty.
  And now I sing, "Any food, any feeding,
  Money, drink or clothing?
  Come dame or maid, be not afraid—
  Poor Tom will injure nothing."
                    —Tom o' Bedlam's Song

IV

IN ONE WAY at least, Parvati reflected as she laid out the various section reports on the table where Hassan would preside over the day's progress meeting, Asgard was almost more suitable for human habitation than Earth. Here, the days were nearly thirty hours long. The twenty-four hours of Earth were—for some unaccountable reason—too short for the natural bio-rhythm of the majority of people; something between twenty-eight and thirty was the cycle that developed under experimental conditions when they were left to find their own preference away from the tyranny of clocks.

They had adjusted gradually as their voyage from home progressed, and everyone had been issued with a watch, on arrival, which kept Asgard instead of Earthly time. Before their first summer was over, virtually everyone was accustomed to the new time-scale—though they sounded a siren for meal-calls, meetings and the midnight curfew, just in case anybody was distracted enough not to keep proper track.

Answering the siren now, people were drifting in steadily from all parts of the island. The first arrivals had gone to the mess-hall and fetched its chairs and benches, ranging them on the level surface of the street facing the chairman's table. Now, with everything ready for the meeting including the computer remotes, Parvati sat down and watched the colonists assembling. Occasionally she waved a greeting.

Almost everyone else was in place before she caught sight of Hassan; she was beginning to worry, wondering why he was delayed. On the basis of the favourable reports she had been reading since breakfast-time, she would have expected the expressions before her to be uniformly contented ones. Instead, she saw a very high proportion of frowns, and there was a distinct trace of nervousness in the way people fidgeted on their seats.

Her relief at seeing Hassan finally approach, from the direction of the ship, lasted only a moment. He was positively scowling, and so was Tai Men, following a couple of paces behind. It was not good for him to be seen with such a look. His moods were contagious.

Seeming to recollect himself with an effort, he smoothed his beak-nosed face with its close-cropped beard into a more neutral expression as he moved around the table to take his place.

"Something wrong?" she whispered under cover of a smile of welcome. Almost without moving his lips, he answered equally softly.

"I'm afraid so. Do we get it out of the way at once or build up the atmosphere with our success story first?"

Parvati weighed the alternatives, wishing that the death of Max Ulfilas aboard the *Pinta* had not robbed her of the insight of the only other person gifted with her particular talents. "Successes first, I think," she said at last. "That is, unless whatever is wrong is going to make us cancel some of the projects which the reports propose?"

"It's not likely to be that bad," Hassan assured her, and rose to confront the colony. Turning in her own chair, Parvati saw that Dennis Malone had appeared at the last moment, as usual, and parked his gangling frame on the extreme end of the rearmost bench.

"Good morning!" Hassan said, his deep voice much too resonant to need the aid of microphones. "This is the fifth of our monthly progress meetings which we've been able to hold out of doors, but I ought to warn you that Kitty says we may have to have the next one in the mess-hall. The fall rains are due to break some time fairly soon, probably in thirty to thirty-five days. But that's about the worst news you have for us, isn't it, Kitty?"

The Greek girl rose, preening herself very slightly as always. "More or less. Temperatures will remain high for probably about another two months, but you'll see from the programme Dan Sakky has prepared that we need to put storm precautions in hand shortly. We're buying our summer comfort for the usual price—the turn of the season is likely to be accompanied by gales which may peak at eighty or ninety miles an hour. However, we can milk them for winter power, I believe. And we designed from the beginning with this risk in mind."

"Dan?" Hassan said.

The big Negro rose in his turn. "Yes, our site here is high enough and sufficiently sheltered by the ridges either side"—he gestured, and heads turned—"to escape the worst we foresee. This morning I've been laying out some boat-sheds down by the harbour, which we can knock together during the next week or two and which will resist any gales. I'm proposing to anchor our houses a little more securely, with guys bedded in heavy concrete blocks, and it looks as though we shall need to fit cyclone shutters over the doors and windows. But in general we ought to ride out the gale period with a minimum of trouble, provided people take the proper care over what they're doing."

"How about the effect on our crops?" Hassan demanded. In answer, Silvana Borelli rose, the husky North Italian girl who specialised in agronomic chemistry and agriculture, one of Tai Men's staff.

"Since we selected crops which normally grow in climatic regions similar to this at home, we don't foresee very serious trouble. We're going to stake and wire the most vulnerable plants, and we're laying out some faired wind-deflectors on the windward slopes. It should be all under control."

"Are the crops coming on satisfactorily?" Hassan asked. Parvati, intently watching the reactions betrayed by their audience, noted a slight tension developing. Hassan knew the answer, of course, and so did she, but it was psychologically better for the colonists at large to hear the spoken assurance of the expert responsible than to read an impersonal written document.

"Yes, the soil is proving perfectly suitable for root and leaf vegetables. It's a trifle early to be sure about the fruits—even the plants we transferred from the ship's own hydroponic trays into the local soil are still showing the shock-effect of the move. But generally speaking all our results are promising, and for the past three weeks a control group of our experimental animals have been living exclusively off native-grown fodder."

Eyebrows rose, and impressed nods made the ranked heads move like grass under a light breeze. Parvati concealed a smile. Trivial little tricks, such as keeping secrets within one specialised section of the community and making announcements like this one, were working magnificently to buoy up the colonists' morale.

So it progressed, through Hassan's own summary of the stores position—better than they had allowed for, so that they were becoming able to divert some of the scrap from the *Niña* to a reserve instead of putting it straight to work—and Ulla's enthusiastic report on mineral resources, to her own psychological report.

Rising, she said, "All I need to do is congratulate you, friends. Maybe you recall, back on Earth, that some people expressed doubts about the ability of our team to start on a new world from scratch. It was said that after so many generations in a technological society, where everyone specialised to the point of depending on millions of others to stay alive, no group as small as ours could make out. Well, we're even smaller than was expected, aren't we?"

That reference to the loss of the *Pinta* was deliberate, too, and produced a stir of reaction.

"And in spite of that," Parvati continued, "we're doing *better* than was expected. Keep it up!"

As she sat down again, she noted that she had provoked precisely the kind of response she wanted: not smugness, but self-approbation.

Now the question remained—was this bad news from Tai Men going to wipe out the good atmosphere the consistent record of success so far had created?

Hassan called on the blocky medical biologist, who got up wearing the same scowl as when he arrived, although it had momentarily disappeared while he was listening to the reports from the other sections.

"Most of you probably know this by now," he said. "We have a problem. It's not—as far as I can tell at the moment—a major setback. But it's indubitably going to be a damned nuisance. Anybody here not know what scurvy is?"

He glanced around. Unable to tell whether everyone knew or not, he amplified.

"It's a deficiency condition, like pellagra and beri-beri. It stems from a shortage of ascorbic acid—what some people still know by the ancient name of vitamin C. When I started getting computer printouts suggesting that was what people were complaining of, a few days ago, I didn't believe it, because we've been eating as balanced a diet since we got here as we were aboard the ships. I think I've finally established why we have the trouble, though.

"Remember we had that epidemic diarrhoea on our

first arrival—a kind of interplanetary *turista?* Well, as you know, most of the bacteria here are used to protoplasm in their hosts which is different enough from ours to mean we can't fall sick from them. However, we always carry around with us certain bacteria from which we don't fall ill, but actually derive benefit. And from analysing and culturing stool-samples we've found that since we got over that diarrhoea epidemic all of us have been carrying around a variety of local bugs which like the hospitable environment of the human bowel. They don't cause any trouble so we needn't bother about them, bar one crucial factor. One of them tends to make ascorbic acid metabolically inaccessible to us. It knocks the molecule about in a way which our bodies aren't accustomed to. So in spite of eating a balanced diet we're developing a deficiency."

Parvati saw with dismay that expressions of gloom—perhaps even of doom—were appearing among the audience. She called out to Tai Men.

"Tai! We can get around this, can't we?"

"Oh, sure, but it'll take time. And scurvy is a very lowering condition. Saps your energy. If we let it spread through the whole colony we're going to fall badly behind schedule. I've set computers to work on the problem of finding a specific to clear these local bugs out of the bowel, but re-infection is inevitable unless we go back to canned air. And although we can stave off the worst effects of the scurvy by taking massive doses of ascorbic acid, our resources of the ready-made are running low and we shan't be capable of such complex chemical synthesis before next spring at the soonest. So I'm afraid it looks as though we're going to have to take a pretty important gamble."

"Spell it out, Tai," Hassan invited.

The biologist drew a deep breath. "We're going to have to switch from hydroponic vegetables to native-grown ones, as soon as possible. It's the only way I can think of to provide the interfering bug with the local chemical for which it's employing our vitamin as a second-best substitute."

V

TAI MEN DIDN'T need to consult Parvati, with whom he inevitably worked more closely than anyone else in the colony simply because the interaction of mind with body made both the psychologist and the medical biologist necessary whenever a complex problem developed—and there had been no shortage of those, despite their all having been solved up until today. He could see for himself that his bombshell had struck deep among his listeners.

Why not? It upsets me pretty badly, too, and I'm supposed to be the dispassionate analyst—the metabolic engineer!

Everyone who had joined the Draco expedition had had to be a specialist; it was essential that the best available skills of Earth should be available to draw on when required. On the other hand, all of the colonists were likewise dilettanti. They had to be able to talk to each other and understand the key concepts in every other discipline besides their own. Well, that was a simple enough matter when it come to doing things like roping in volunteer help to string power and phone lines. You couldn't live on modern Earth without using powergrids and communications networks.

But faced with the idea that this awareness inside the skull—this ego, this creature called "I"—actually depended on processes which could be extracted and isolated in a lab experiment, most people tended to shy off. While being dutifully aware of the way in which potassium cyanide halted metabolism, or the carriage of oxygen by the oxyhaemoglobin of the red cells, they still preferred in the ultimate resort to think in subjective terms: "hungry, I eat; tired, I rest."

Cogito, ergo sum.

It was one thing to come out of the sanctuary of the ship, peel down the soft bark layers of a woodplant, saw the harder xylem beneath into planks and beams which could be dried stiffly into place and form shelters. That was akin to going camping, a sort of flirtation with the primitive, and implied adventure. It overlaid the crude facts of survival with a gloss of play.

But when it came to risking the delicate balance of their very bodies on the assurance of someone whose data they could not fully understand, it was different.

Yet, for all he had struggled to find one, he could propose no alternative to the suggestion he had already voiced. The crash of the *Pinta* had deprived the colony of irreplaceable biological resources. Each ship's computer memories had been assigned a speciality, and what survived included little more than an abstract of certain key areas of modern biophysical knowledge. Similarly, although each ship had been allotted a complete cross-section of essential equipment, so that if two ships had been lost the crew of the third could live in the remaining ship and tackle the problem of moving out on the new world's surface by slow degrees, no one of the three was intended to carry out the complete job at the original rate. There simply wasn't any cargo capacity. The colony was likely to have to survive independently of help from Earth for about a century; it would take that long, said the economists, to make up the fantastic drain on terrestrial resources caused by the first expedition. You could have built fifty cities with the materials absorbed in the project; you could have populated an ancient empire with the people who became directly or indirectly involved.

That meant that a choice between duplicating a certain item of equipment or including another couple in the crew must always be resolved in favour of the crew. To spread out and populate the new world without risking the consequences of inbreeding, the colonists needed a gene-pool as large as could be made available. And so far tectogenetic modification was only an experimental technique, not one which people struggling to stay alive on an alien world could expect to be employing within one generation.

On the other hand—and here he shared the instant, frightened resentment of the non-biologists who had heard his explanation—it seemed incredibly frustrating that an organism far too small to be visible should now threaten their success not with some spectacular illness, but simply with a process of undermining their welfare.

It would be intolerable to see the vigour and enthusiasm of the colonists drained away by the insidious leech of scurvy. But at the edge of his mind the shadow lurked, which was Death. He was as sure as he could be that Earthly plants grown in Asgard soil contained a substance which would negate the impact of the local bacterium on the human metabolism. It didn't really want ascorbic acid; that was merely the compound which came most readily to it in a human gut. It was more accustomed to utilise a chemical analogue which human digestion passed through the system, disregarded.

But there were many, many possible compounds which the interaction of Earthly vegetables with Asgard soil might produce, and he lacked the stored computer-data which would have listed them for him—or rather, for the computer which he could later have asked whether they would also affect human metabolism. So far none of the control animals fed on locally grown plants had shown signs of disease, but a man was not a pig or a rat.

He said harshly, "I think we shall have to call for volunteers!"

There was a long pause. Parvati winced, but only on the inside of her mind, wishing Tai had consulted her before making the announcement. The pivotal psychological element of their success, it seemed to her, was the way they had totally eliminated conflict among the group; they were all collaborators in a single venture. Splitting them into "test subjects" and "others" could easily be disastrous. *Any* division implied a threat. Always hovering over her estimates and predictions there loomed the stormcloud of what had happened to Dennis Malone on his first visit to Asgard—that instant of insanity which might have killed him and Sigrid by letting in infection, or poison. That it had not done so made no difference in principle. And there was Dennis himself, now, rising to his feet, thrusting his fingers through his tousled brown hair, almost defiantly addressing the rest of the audience.

"Sure, I'll volunteer!"

Martyr complex. Parvati nudged Hassan, whose skill in controlling the massed individualities of the colony was instinctive rather than trained, and found he was already rapping for attention.

"Just a moment, Dennis," he said mildly, and continued, addressing Tai. "You'll have to give us a few more data, I'm afraid, before we can reasonably decide on that proposal of yours. Have you asked the computers to weigh the alternatives?"

"Yes, naturally." Tai wiped his face with a fluttering handkerchief. "Unfortunately the incidence of this scurvy has gone from zero ten days ago to twenty-two cases today. That's a rate of increase which they are ordered to regard as a major threat. So they recommend diverting our entire resources to eliminating the bacterium and synthesising ascorbic acid. Which of course we can't do. Not without the *Pinta*."

One or two people were starting to tremble, Parvati's keen gaze informed her. This was worse than she had anticipated.

"The next best possibility is the one I've mentioned," Tai went on. "That's to supplement our diet with the native-grown plants. But I can't hide the element of risk which doing that entails. Some animals, as you heard, are now living exclusively off local fodder without visible ill effects. But this has only been the case for three weeks, and there are compounds which accumulate in the body, and we—well, again thanks to the loss of the *Pinta*, we need to keep alive as many of the test animals as possible, for breeding, so we can't kill enough of them to carry out daily analyses of their tissue. We're relying on blood and serum samples mainly, which are excellent in their way, but not infallible."

"How long before we run out of ready-made ascorbic acid?" Hassan demanded.

"I don't want to run out," Tai grunted. "I want to keep enough in reserve to tide us over the winter, when we may not be able to go out and gather even hardy leaf-vegetables, let alone citrus fruits or any other highly concentrated sources of the stuff. And that means we ought to start supplementing our diet at once."

"I said I'd volunteer!" Dennis Malone called out again, and several people frowned at him for interrupting. Parvati was debating whether to cut in herself, when Ulla spoke up with admirable timeliness.

"I need you to go and find me some diamonds, Dennis! I told you this morning! Tai, while I'm on my feet: can't you locate a native source of this compound which we might extract—say, with some of our fractional distillation rigs?"

"We may be able to," Tai Men conceded. "But I don't think there's any hope of getting the quantities we'd need. In your terms, I guess it would be as difficult as separating a rare-earths sample, perhaps even worse because since this damnable local bug can use ascorbic acid, the native compound is chemically very close indeed to it. If only it were close enough for us to utilise it too . . . But it's not. We're more complicated organisms; we're much more choosy."

"Shall I assign you some fractionating columns anyway?" Ulla offered.

"Yes!"

The single word came from Hassan, before Tai Men could answer.

"Tai, as a matter of policy, we're going to exhaust every other alternative before we start risking irreplaceable human lives on this problem." Very stern, very paternal, Hassan glowered across the close-packed audience towards the biologist. "And that goes for your offer, too, Dennis!" he added sharply. "I'm sure everyone admires and appreciates it, but it's premature. This is an order, Tai: you're to do your best to isolate concentrated ascorbic acid, free from any local contaminant, from the Earthly plants you've got growing. You're also to go out and test every promising local plant to see whether ascorbic acid occurs here naturally along with the compound which you say is analogous to it. I'm not a specialist, but that seems conceivable to me."

Tai Men gave a grudging shrug.

"Give me the equipment I'll need to make the right tests, and I'll see if I can find some in another climatic zone," Dennis called. "I'm going off to find Ulla's diamonds—I might as well make the most of the chance."

"Yes, certainly," Hassan nodded. "In fact, I think we'd better declare this a priority. Co-opt anyone who can be spared from the other sections, Tai, show them how to make the tests, and if you don't come up with anything on this island, see what you can locate on islands a bit further afield."

"It may not help much," Tai said dampingly.

"Why not?"

"This place is like Earth in that once a particular compound has been shown to fill a metabolic niche, it tends to recur whenever the equivalent need arises again. Some of the local counterparts of vitamins run clear through the biological gamut from unicellular bacteria to large mobile animals. If organisms exist here which use ascorbic acid by choice, they'll be relatively as rare as—well, let's say creatures on Earth which use copper instead of iron in their blood."

He shrugged. "One can't have it both ways. The fact that there's this marginal chemical difference between the local life-forms and ourselves means that we don't immediately catch all the infectious bacteria and viruses there are going. On the other hand . . . *this*."

He sat down, and as though a cloud had crossed the sun Parvati felt the chill of anticipated doom settle on the assembly.

IV

COMPELLED BY HER speciality to think about the deep implications of such phenomena, Parvati had always regarded it as a promising sign that the colony had developed a few of its own customs almost directly after the landing. When the reports rendered to the first monthly progress meeting showed that nothing had gone seriously wrong, a celebration had developed spontaneously. The next month, it had been repeated because people had so much enjoyed the first one, and thereafter it was a tradition.

Under the stringent conditions of shipboard life, there had been little opportunity for simply enjoying oneself. Finding that the reservoir of relaxation could be tapped so easily, she had been pleased. It would be an excellent augury for the colony's stability if, instead of carrying over Earthly festivals, the settlers were to develop their own from such simple beginnings.

Not until this evening had she entertained the idea that celebrations established by tradition themselves masked a subtle danger.

Like its predecessors, this took the form of a party, a little different from an Earthly party but not much. There was a minimum of alcohol or any other drug—if, despite all their precautions, someone with a latent tendency to alcoholism had slipped through the psychological net they had used to sift the volunteers, he or she might too easily die when drunk merely because of not knowing Asgard instinctively. The same went for the popular mild hallucinogens and other aids to merriment. But there was plenty of good food, over which the kitchen staff had spent several hours, and there were various juices and light wines which could be produced in quantity from their hydroponic fruits, and there was home-made entertainment ranging from the formal chamber music of the string quartet led by Ulla Berzelius, through the electronic colour-music which had been a lifetime hobby for Saul Carpender, their shipwright, to her own repertoire of ancient Indian temple dances performed before a light gauze screen on which were back-projected pictures of the temples at

Konarak and Kajuraho, symbols of the power of man's handiwork to survive against the random incursions of Nature.

Tonight, though, she hoped to avoid being called on to perform. It seemed that her hope was going to be fulfilled. It was still early, but there were fewer couples than usual dancing on the level section of their single street which they used for their parties. She had the impression that, as always, they were slipping away to make love—which was a good thing, in the sense that the planners of the colony had realised promiscuity must be made a virtue for the sake of mixing the gene-pool they disposed of when it came time to start their first pregnancies, and a bad thing because it brought back to her mind the curious experience which Dennis had undergone on his first visit to Asgard, when he found himself overcome by lust for Sigrid.

Neither Sigrid nor Carmen had consented to accompany the colonists. But that wasn't really surprising. Both of them, after their fantastic adventure, had been able to choose from a thousand or more eligible prospective husbands, and uncountable generations of natural selection had ensured that the male sex of humanity was temperamentally the more inclined to rove.

Music recorded far away on Earth welled from the speakers hung under the eaves of the nearest houses. A little soothed by it, despite her worries, Parvati looked around and realised that Dennis had come to sit a few places away from her along the row of chairs which fronted the mess-hall. On impulse, she said, "Dennis, do you believe the theory we psychologists dreamed up to explain what happened to you and Sigrid?"

He stared at her blankly for a moment, and she was afraid she had offended him. Suddenly, however, his day-long look of veiled depression vanished, and he grinned.

"Well, well, *well!* I never thought the day would arrive when a shrinker would ask me whether she was right!"

A little crossly, she said, "Please, Dennis, we're in a terrible corner, you know. Talk about the observer affecting the results—we *are* the results, aren't we?"

Looking contrite, he moved to take the chair next to her and laid his hand briefly on her knee. "I'm sorry," he muttered. "Yes, I do appreciate what a load you're carrying. It makes us—well, you might almost say it makes us colleagues, doesn't it? After all, we're the only two people who are carrying unique loads."

She pondered that for a second, then saw what he meant. "Yes, I guess we are," she agreed. "Though if I still had Max Ulfilas to turn to . . ."

"And if I still had Pyotr."

The words hung heavy on the warm evening air. He ended the pause by saying in a brisker tone, "Do I believe the suggestion that Sigrid and I needed to put some kind of symbolic mark on this planet by making love on one of its beaches? I suppose I do." He was frowning as he spoke. "After all, there are two points which at the time worried me terribly. The first was that this wasn't the kind of casual coupling we'd enjoyed on the way out, and there'd been plenty of those, although I preferred Carmen and she Pyotr. We liked the occasional change well enough. But this was . . ."

"Unique?"

"Of course. And that's the second point. When we came back to the ship and admitted rather shamefacedly to Carmen and Pyotr what we'd done—I say 'we' because although I'd started it she was overtaken by the same need within a few minutes—then, of course, there was the dreadful period of anxiety while they made certain we hadn't picked up a germ or poisoned ourselves or anything. But later on, because the work-schedule demanded it, Pyotr and Carmen were away from the ship together for much longer than Sigrid and I had been. And they never felt the same impulse. It was as though once was enough. But that once was indispensable."

There was another pause. During it Parvati found herself looking at him speculatively, and he diagnosed the thoughts which lay behind her expression with unerring accuracy. He touched her leg again.

"I'm sorry, Parvati. You're a lovely woman, but—but I feel doomed to be alone for a while longer yet."

With an effort she recovered her detachment. She said, "Yes, Dennis. And in spite of what I said to you this morning, please don't think that I don't recognise what a tremendous amount of effort it's costing you to damp down your frustration. It must be pure hell to find yourself among so many other people who have got exactly what they want, when you never wanted it in your life."

"I couldn't have put it more neatly myself," Dennis said with a wry twist of his mouth. He hesitated. "I think I may get over it, though, provided I can manage to give the right sops to the Cerberus of my subconscious by going off on trips like the one I'm going to start tomorrow for Ulla. I know I shan't ever be able to indulge my urge to explore on the scale I was used to when I was—well, *before*. But I guess maybe I can learn to make do with half a loaf. There is one thing I've been meaning to ask you, though."

"Ask away."

"It's hard to put into words, but what it amounts to is this: Asgard sprang a trap on me once, when this really was an alien planet and there were only two couples here. Are there likely to be any other traps, when there are hundreds or maybe even thousands of people here?"

"Yes," Parvati said. "But who can say what they will be?"

Dennis licked his lips and glanced around to see whether anyone else might have overheard the remark. Parvati had timed it, however, for a moment when a dance had ended and the couples nearby had started to surge towards the bar. He said, "Thanks. I don't suppose that's a point you make to many of us."

"It's good to hear you say 'us'," Parvati countered dryly. "But you're right, of course. The information to draw the conclusion exists and is available. But we shall have to work our way through a lot of tribal stages, including the one where you have an in-group which constitutes a repository of traditional wisdom, before we can attempt the kind of free educational structure that exists on Earth. You see why?"

"For all our skills, the scale of what we're trying to do dwarfs us to the condition of Bushmen," Dennis said. "And I include myself, and say 'us', because I'm the odd-job man in our microcosmic culture. True or false?"

"True."

"So what are these traps most likely to consist in? I was victim of one, and since I'm not getting my heart's desire by being here, I might well be victim of another."

Parvati turned her large dark eyes upward. Tonight the moon was not yet high enough to be seen over the nearby roofs; there were only the stars overhead.

"The kind we've guarded against, with luck. Two kinds, rather. Being dwarfed exemplifies one of them. But we've made such headway with the sort of tools a single pair of hands can wield, we ought very rapidly to get away from the risk that we can be caved in and made to despair by the sheer size of the project we've undertaken. Ideally, if we were reduced to an Adam and Eve, they wouldn't need to quit; they could still hope to establish humanity permanently on Asgard. But the ideal case won't arise, of course—though something like it might."

"Yes. Well, if it was the scale of a whole new world which affected me and Sigrid, that's a point I can understand." Dennis rubbed his chin. "What's the second kind of danger?"

"The second kind of precaution, you mean," Parvati corrected. "Why, you gave an example yourself just now, when you mentioned the Cerberus of your subconscious. We don't know precisely what kind of cultural frame a human being needs to keep his sanity. At best we can make enlightened guesses. That's why we brought as much personal contact with as many areas of Earthly tradition as we could arrange. You had this before the first expedition, didn't you?"

"Sigrid reciting from the Kalevala-when none of the rest of us spoke a word of Finnish! Sure we did. But . . ." Dennis broke off. "Hell, of course! Before the trip was out, I'd learned enough to understand most of it, and I'd taught her to carry on a simple conversation in Erse. And Pyotr used to tell us stories from *Igor's Campaign* . . . Is that why you're a dancer?"

"Naturally. Hadn't it struck you before?"

"Not quite in that way. I mean, of course I'd recognised the value of having creative and artistic people along, but I'd assumed it was only to guard against boredom. You're implying it's guarding against something more serious."

"There isn't anything more serious than boredom, Dennis. Not when you have to concentrate every waking hour of your life on not doing things which came automatically to you at home, because you don't yet know if they're safe." Parvati made a gesture as though trying to seize an example from the air. "Ah yes! You like to swim, don't you?"

"Very much."

"I thought so. Almost all spacemen do. But would you walk down that beach now and into the warm, clear ocean?"

Dennis shook his head vigorously. "I'd love to. I won't until Tai says it's safe. But the temptation has been pretty fierce lately. Is that what you mean when you say there's nothing worse than boredom?"

"Of course. Coming from a leisured society as we do, we're used to certain activities which keep up our interest in being alive. Here, some of them are going to have to wait; meantime we must make do with work, and our work is going so incredibly well we may even have to advance the schedule and over-extend ourselves simply because we know the work is safe while the play may not be."

She sighed. "It's wearing, but it has to be done!"

Dennis looked at her thoughtfully for long seconds. Suddenly he said, "Parvati, come with me tomorrow."

She smiled. "Dennis, I'd like to very much. But I can't. Things are going to get very difficult here for the next few weeks, thanks to this scurvy problem Tai turned up. I'll be needed. But I'd like to come to your room with you now, if that's okay."

Dennis kept his eyes fixed on her face. In a tone of near despair he said, "I wish it could be okay. But I'm afraid it wouldn't be. You see . . . Well, whether it's due to the first time it happened here or not, it doesn't seem as though it could mean anything unless it was part of my striking roots on Asgard, and that means it's got to be tied up with doing the only thing I can find to do here. If anyone can understand that, you must. Good night, Parvati."

THREE   NOT SINCE THE CONQUEST

With a thought I took for Maudlin
And a cruse of cockle pottage,
With a thing thus tall (sky bless you all)
I fell into this dotage.
I slept not since the conquest—
Till then I never wakéd
Till the roguish boy of love where I lay
Me found and stripped me naked
  And made me sing, "Any food, any feeding,
  Money, drink or clothing?
  Come dame or maid, be not afraid—
  Poor Tom will injure nothing."
                    —Tom o' Bedlam's Song

VII

ONLY SAUL CARPENDER, the rangy Australian who had been selected as their shipwright and harbourmaster because his long experience of wandering around the islands of the Pacific had prepared him for conditions on Asgard, was at the little natural wharf next morning to see Dennis off. But he was in the forefront of the minds of many, many other people.

Paradoxically, they were jealous of him.

The planners of the Asgard colony had always taken the worst assumptions for granted when deciding what equipment to stock the ships with. It was far faster to move around any planet through its atmosphere rather than in contact with its land and water surfaces, so they might have opted for two or three compact, powerful airplanes or helicopters to furnish the colony with long-range transport. Instead they provided cushionfoils. Between island and island they could speed along on their underwater wings, and if necessary they could cross land or sandbars by means of their hoverducts. But most important of all, if their engines failed they could be stripped of their foils and still serve for inter-island transport with oars or sails. It was not by any means certain that the colonists could pass on working engines to their descendants, but seamanship *must* be passed on because it could equally be applied to a dug-out canoe.

Spacemanship, on the other hand, could wait—as Dennis had often cynically reminded himself. Possibly the *Santa Maria* might lift to space again, to explore the nearer planets. But if a ship went from here to Earth again in his lifetime, it would be owing to an irremediable disaster.

Is there any point to all this, really? So there are human beings under two suns instead of one: so what?

But the impulses which led human beings off on crazy ventures like this were too far below the conscious level for even the finest modern psychologists to do more than hint at explanations.

He finished checking the long manifest he had compiled for himself by adding Ulla's and Tai's new requirements to the one for his last trip and striking off what he had no need for this time. His boat, rocking gently on the outgoing tide, was mostly engine and cargo space anyway, and he had put in every possible additional item against emergencies that the spare passenger space could hold, as well. Successful explorers had vivid and pessimistic imaginations, or so he had always found. But he wasn't taking anything which might be indispensable back here on the base island, apart from the jar of vitamin capsules Tai Men had insisted on slipping into his medikit. Since the alarming discovery that scurvy had already broken out, the biologist had become almost obsessed with deficiency diseases, and was ordering a complete check of their diet.

"How long are you going to be away?" Saul demanded, after a long thoughtful study of the loaded boat.

Dennis shrugged. "As long as seems to be useful. I'll keep in radio contact, of course. I arranged with Abdul to do the same as before—call up every evening at meal-time. And there'll be a monitor on my frequency as well, naturally."

"A week? Two weeks? A month?" Saul seemed to want a firm answer. Surprised, Dennis resorted to jocularity.

"Going to miss me, or something? That's nice! But

let's just say that if you go ahead with Dan's boat-sheds along here, I'm not likely to recognise the harbour when I get back."

Saul didn't respond to his light tone. He said with a sudden uncharacteristic burst of frankness, "Wish I could cut loose like that!"

"Why—?" Dennis had been about to say: "Why on earth?" He cancelled it, and substituted: "Why in the world?"

"Oh! I don't know." Saul shrugged helplessly. "I guess—yes, maybe this is why. If it was something I could do something about which had suddenly gone wrong with our plans, I wouldn't be worried. I'd just buckle to and sort the problem out. Hell, we lost the *Pinta,* didn't we? And you saw what happened: everyone sort of cursed the universe and put twice as much energy into everything to get their own back. But this scurvy bit is different. It's something I only knew of as a word in a history book, before now."

Pounding fist into palm, he concluded, "It's ridiculous! Everything is going better than we expected bar this one thing which hasn't even done us serious harm yet, and very well may not do harm at all—and here I am with my skin practically crawling! Does it hit you that way?"

"I guess it does," Dennis admitted. "But I wish you hadn't told me how you're feeling. I hoped it was just me."

High up on the skeletal web of naked girders which had been the bones of the *Niña*—still were, though now grotesquely revolting because they were being systematically flayed of their hull-skin—Abdul Hassan saw the plume of steam that rose when Dennis fired the engines of his boat. He paused in the conversation he was having, which concerned the problem of which cannibalised parts should be held in reserve, which put straight to work, and repressed an unexpected shiver.

Tibor Gyorgy, who was responsible for their electronics systems, said in alarm, "Something wrong, Abdul?"

With some effort, the colony's chairman recovered his self-possession. "No, nothing," he lied, and went on talking in a perfectly normal tone. But behind the mask he was wishing there could be a way out for him, as there was for Dennis—wishing, in effect, that he was not indispensable.

All right, so it's wonderful to be here on a strange new planet and find that outwardly it's kindly, gentle, hospitable . . . But that's only the way it looks. We know that it may injure us in some way we can't suspect because we never lived on another planet before, at least not without canned air, spacegear, big obvious dangers like vacuum. So we must think, think, think and never ever stop!

How long can a human being manage to burden his mind with the need to make a conscious decision about every action he undertakes, even about his next breath? And I of all people dare not make even a single error.

I'm in a trap, and I don't know what the trap is. I only know it's there.

They had chosen Parvati Chandra for the colony, and Max Ulfilas who was dead, because they were not simply psychologists. They both had a rare, perhaps unprecedented, gift for extracting the pattern of a trend from actions they could see still going on. Asgard was sure to evolve its own kind of society, different from any on Earth—although since the raw material was human, there would be resemblances. It was necessary to provide that society with a sociology that did not need the hindsight of history to know when it had gone astray.

Crossing a ridge on her way to one of the experimental vegetable-plots, she glanced back and saw Dennis's boat as it rose on its foils after leaving the harbour. For an instant she was overwhelmed by a vain desire: that she could have accepted his invitation of last night to go with him on his exploring trip.

But I couldn't desert the colony when it faces its first major crisis . . . Yet I want to. I want to desperately!

Dispassionately, she considered for the first time whether she might not have to recommend the abandonment of Asgard, and whether she could cope with the hysterical resentment of the would-have-been settlers.

Tai Men was again taking the morning sick call at the entrance to the *Santa Maria*'s main lock. There were no new cases of scurvy today, and naturally all those to whom he had administered massive doses of ascorbic acid were instantly on the mend. But there remained the risk that no way would be found to cope with the recurrence of this trouble, or the development of another like it. In which case the resentment of the colonists would devolve on him, because the cause of their failure would lie in his area of responsibility.

I wish I could duck out like Dennis, Tai Men thought. *And come back in a month's time to find the problem solved . . .*

For Kitty Minakis, launching the usual batch of high-altitude radiosondes, the envy she felt on noticing Dennis's boat stemmed chiefly from boredom. Once, long ago, she had thoroughly enjoyed the speciality to which she had committed her mathematical talents; she was a brilliant mental calculator capable of handling even such complex independent variables as were involved in weather forecasting with minimum recourse to computers.

But she had mastered that. Centuries of gathering information about Earth's weather had reduced prediction to almost an exact discipline. She had offered herself for Asgard in the hope of finding new, tougher challenges.

Instead, she had found Asgard's weather ridiculously simple. It was closer to the ideal case of a water-covered globe than Earth, hence everything was less complex.

Sighing, she wished she could escape, even for a few days, from what was becoming a dull, repetitious job.

Dan Sakky had seized gladly on the chance of assigning two of his team to help Tai Men, and today, in place of one of them, he was driving a powerdozer and levelling foundations. Getting to grips with the basics of his job—that was what he needed. He wanted the resistance of rock, the dull stolidity of clay. He would almost have preferred to be using a pick and shovel.

Pausing to watch Dennis's boat as it skimmed towards the horizon, he wished that he too could find a brief respite. He had spent too long with abstracts, and abstracts were soft, easy, frustrating. Already in his spare time he had designed a gloriously functional city to occupy this island, capable of housing and servicing half a million people in enormous comfort. But all that was a game.

And, although it was certainly good to wrestle with the obdurate material he used for his creations, at the back of his mind sniggered the suspicion that it might all go for nothing because the people to use what he built might be too sick to enjoy what he gave them. Over that, as a construction man, he had no control.

* * *

Standing on the dam which held back their reservoir of fresh water, Ulla Berzelius glanced up from the dials of her portable analyser, and spotted Dennis's boat as it vanished. She had just discovered that the indium she was looking for was present in adequate quantities.

Hell! What's the use of a world which gives you exactly what you think you want, then takes away, mocking, something you didn't know you needed? I wish I could be going off like Dennis, not in search of these damned dull minerals that we already knew from the astronomers must exist, but looking for jewels—enormous, lovely, absolutely useless jewels!

I wonder how many more of us are sick of things we need, and desperate for things we'd simply enjoy.

VIII

THE COMPUTERS HAD furnished Dennis with a shortest course taking in all the promising areas where the local geology hinted at diamond deposits. It had also indicated that by following the tide-run he could keep his time away from the island down to a maximum of nine days.

Perversely, he elected to follow the charted course in precisely the opposite direction. He felt that if he could not stretch his absence to the point where before he turned for home he was hungry for company, he was never going to rid himself of his craving for Earth.

Isn't it curious that the explorer, not the settlers, should be homesick?

Resting easily in the open cockpit of the boat, its foils holding it level four feet above the peaks of the gentle summer waves, he considered that paradox, and decided that it wasn't a paradox at all. Asgard was a very beautiful world—more so than Earth, indeed, for man's callousness and stupidity had not raped its plains into deserts nor smeared its rich valleys with ugly, monotonous townscapes. He yearned symbolically for Earth simply because that was the place from which he had set out, the place where he had been given the chance to gratify his explorer's urge. Exploration for its own sake was a luxury Asgard would not be able to afford for generations.

And yet . . .

He thought about the people among whom he was seemingly stranded for the rest of his life, when he had meant at most to spend a year with them and then return taking whichever of them had proved unable to endure the stress of the new world. Was he not fortunate to have escaped that duty? By the time they caved in and abandoned their self-respect to the point of creeping home, whipped-dog-fashion, the failed colonists would have been abominable travelling companions, most likely needing to be kept tranked to their eyeballs for the entire duration of the voyage.

And were these people not as stimulating, as intelligent, as talented, as might have been found in any city on Earth to which he could have retired? Maybe more so, for in a city they would be diluted among a vast horde of nonentities, needing to be sought out and put in touch with one another, whereas here they were concentrated and united.

Yes, all that is true. But somehow it doesn't reach me where it counts.

He felt he was groping towards the recognition of an important truth, which perhaps no one else among the colonists except Parvati would have reached. The day was bright and warm again, with a breeze just vigorous enough to cream the occasional wavetop into foam, so that the deep emerald sea was touched with a veining of white, as though it were all one flowing gemstone; the sun gleamed on the polished nodules of the woodplants which decorated the crowns of the nearby islands, a rich red-brown between the colours of mahogany and sequoia-bark, and lay like warm syrup among the close-set shrubs and bushes which filled the intervening valleys. To many human beings, could they have been snatched forward from barbarous ages in the past, the mere sight would have suggested paradise.

And still ought to. Only . . .

The formulation of the concept he sensed, but could not pin down, was like trying to mould wisps of smoke into a statue. Sighing, he made the usual automatic check of his instruments and found nothing was wrong—that also being usual—before starting a fresh attempt to sort out his ideas.

He spread out one of his charts across his knees and studied it, because of a point which looking at the nearby islands had brought to mind.

I wonder if our skills are too great? It took men a hundred thousand years to go from grunts and fire-hardened sticks to adequate maps of their home planet. This map took about a hundred hours: photographs from space, collated to eliminate the fuzziness which cloud-cover imposed on the image, converted automatically into contoured equivalents, and printed by the score.

And yet that wasn't what he was after, either. The skills of any given moment were the product of human thinking, whether they were on the Neolithic level or the Nuclear. His voyage in the *Argo* was about as remarkable, in perspective, as the travels of its legendary namesake, although, given modern longevity treatments, he had devoted less of his lifespan to his travels than those ancient Greeks.

On the other hand, of course, one might argue that

the scale of the challenges men faced had not kept pace with their ingenuity. He glanced up from the map to identify an island which, by his chart, should just be passing on his starboard side, and noticed how very closely it resembled the one where men had settled. This he had been struck by on his first visit, though. When they moved about the planet's surface, staying briefly in each of the climatic zones from polar to tropical in order to assess the habitability of each, they had chosen their landing-sites more or less randomly within each zone.

There was much less variety here than on Earth, one had to concede that, even though the total effect was un-Earthly. For instance, their base island was hexagonal and spined with ridges radiating from a central peak; the contours on the chart he held made it look like an X-ray photograph of an Earthly sea-star.

But so was that island yonder, whose appearance he had just glanced up to verify. The lines suggested by the ridges of one could be traced across the seabed to the termini of others like them on another island. There was a web of wrinkles all over the planet, and wherever you went you found much the same physical features shading gradually from one area to another. Under the sea, of course, one inevitably found a geology more like Earth's. But men were surface-living creatures. They could learn from their submarine survey remotes that the equivalent of continents existed on Asgard; with their own eyes and the touch of their bare hands, however, they could detect only a sort of vast Pacific. There was not even an Australia to provide contrast; the largest island on the whole planet was smaller than Britain.

Now, he realised, he was getting somewhere with his meditations. It was a wonderful thing to conquer a whole new world under an alien sun by the pure power of reason—analysing, testing, drawing conclusions, and acting on them—but for him at least the mere solving of problems was not enough justification to stay alive. When all the factors were known before you committed yourself, no external influence could surprise you. He remembered Kitty Minakis rising at their first monthly progress meeting, the only one they had held inside the ship, to answer some questions about the weather the colony would have to contend with. She had said something to the effect that the temperature of Asgard was not actually higher than Earth's, in the sense that its distance from the sun gave it a comparable quantity of solar radiation. But owing to the seasonal nature of the icecaps, less heat was reflected from snow and ice, and the annual melting produced little more than an aberration in the ocean temperature—it didn't give rise to huge cold currents like the polar waters of Earth.

What was the image she used? "The typical polar phenomenon here is not snow, as it is at home, but merely fog."

There was something definite about snow: water after a change of state, abruptly differentiated into white flakes. But fog was merely a clammy nuisance.

Somewhere in there was—

The boat changed course abruptly, snatching him out of his brown study and back to awareness. Instantly he was alert to danger, one hand slapping down to the pocket where he kept his bolt-gun, the other poised to hit the emergency manual controls. There was no need. All that had happened was that the sonar had detected a large water-creature surfacing from the bottom— here, there was a channel nearly five hundred feet deep—and swerved to miss it.

Excited, he saw it as it broke amid a vast bubble, a burp of stored air which it had used to go gathering its food on the lowermost slopes of the submarine mountains among which it roved. He had seen such a beast before, though only once, and swung his camera for Yoko to catch a few seconds of it before it had drawn a fresh breath and vanished.

Now if only I were a xenobiologist . . . I can't imagine Yoko losing her interest in this world before she's very old.

Why were there air-breathing herbivores in the oceans of this watery world? During what glacial period had their ancestors abandoned gills for lung-equivalents, and what upheaval had subsequently driven them back, like Earthly whales, to browse with their enormous comb-like lips on the deep-sea plants? Although the tumult on the water had lasted only moments, his memory retained the vivid picture of the beast: a thing like a carrot, to use a crude but exact comparison, frilled around its body with dozens of fins, bearing specialised sense-organs ranging from pressure-detectors to olfactory glands, its mouth where an Earthly creature's tail would be, furnished with lips which served the double purpose of flukes and food-gatherers, upon which the comb-like serrations could open and shut as the feathers of a bird's wing do.

Fascinating!

But his excitement was superficial. Sighing, settling back in his seat as the boat automatically resumed its course, he admitted to himself that what he felt on seeing that alien beast come charging up for air was exactly what a hunter might have felt on spotting his first elephant. Beyond the—well, literally, the *fun* of seeing it, what was there to gratify him? Merely the re-counting of a fabulous tale to envious stay-at-homes. His temperament had never involved him in what he had imagined, a minute earlier, as furnishing Yoko with a lifetime interest: the patient dissection of a whole new biological system.

Naturally, before being sent here for the first time, he like all his companions had been taught to use the instruments with which the *Argo* was equipped, and those included biological analysers. After their five months' stay, at least half of what they now knew about Asgard's animal and vegetable life had already been established, or at least could be guessed with reasonable certainty by comparing it with Earth's. Gathering this huge mass of data, though, had been a matter of rote-following for him. It was the computers that took it in and understood it. All he did was feed them.

He knew a little about a vast number of subjects. The first visitors to Asgard might have been confronted with any sort of emergency from man-eating monsters to plague. They might even have wrecked their ship and been compelled to colonise the planet involuntarily. Accordingly, they had to have a grasp of the outline of any given area of knowledge, so that they could ask the proper questions when they needed to extract more specific guidance from the computers—or guess.

But knowing a little about many subjects was dilettantism. He had no all-absorbing passion to satisfy him. He was an observer, an explorer, a . . .

"Hell, I'm a *tourist!*" he said to the uncaring air. And, as though that fit of gloomy cynicism had somehow relieved his intolerable mental burden, he turned to break out his noon meal from the rack of cartons behind his seat. By this evening he would have reached the first island which promised a chance of diamonds, according to the computers.

It would be good to have work to do, real genuine valuable work which would contribute to the welfare and success of the colony. It would buy him a sort of personal stake.

But finding diamonds wouldn't be what he needed. He wouldn't know a diamond in the uncut state if he kicked it on the path! The credit would belong to Ulla and the computers!

Ripping the top from his meal-carton with a savage gesture, he muttered, "I never dreamed anybody—I or anybody else—could wind up in a state where everything was going perfectly and he was going out of his mind with frustration in spite of it!"

IX

IT FELT VERY strange to come back inside the ship after living for so long in the village below, Parvati noticed. No sooner had she become aware of the reaction than her mind was away in search of possible reasons.

It was as though she were being screened from exterior reality, perhaps, as a metal box will screen a receiver from a broadcast. And, of course, there were metal boxes around her—from the hull of the ship itself successively reducing to the scale of the automatic elevator which was carrying her up to the computer levels, with its padded walls of a soothing dark blue.

The ship is of Earth, she reasoned. *It seems marginally unreal, because Earth is out of reach for good and all.*

The elevator stopped. Waiting to enter it and go down was Yoko, clutching a thick wad of computer printouts. They exchanged greetings, and Parvati walked forward across the floor of the computer-room. It had been the bridge too, when the ship was in flight, and someone had draped cloths over the astrogation inputs.

She frowned at that; it was new since she last came up here. It was an irrational deed, in the sense that it was superfluous—everyone knew that the flight-controls were there, but no longer for use.

Who did it? Who acted on the principle, "If you can't see it, maybe it will go away"?

Over the past few days, since the progress meeting, it seemed that an infinite multitude of such trivial—but irrational—facts had been accumulating in the corner of her memory which stored them until they generated a suggestive pattern. Ordinarily, when she had gathered so many, she settled down to puzzle over them whenever she had the chance. At present, however, she was curiously reluctant to face them.

If she had found herself alone up here, she might nonetheless have attempted the job immediately: punched the computer-activation code which alerted those sections of the memory stocked with information about human aberrations, and tossed every petty irritation she could think of into a heap from which the computers might have drawn some conclusions.

She was not alone. Seated before the section of the input board which dealt with his own speciality, Tai Men was studying a printout with such concentration he did not realise she had come in until she spoke to him.

Then he jerked and glanced over his shoulder. "Oh—morning, Parvati. How are things with you?"

"So-so. But better than with you, to judge by the expression you're wearing." She unlocked a chair with a touch on its back, slid it across the smooth metal floor to a spot where she could conveniently talk to him, and released the switch so that it stayed put.

"I'm afraid you're right," the biologist said unhappily. "Ah—has it been showing very much, these past few days?"

"I don't know what you mean by 'very much.' But it has been showing," Parvati said candidly.

Tai Men sighed. "Yes, I thought so. And it isn't good for morale, is it? But what I've run into is a pretty good excuse for paranoia, I guess . . . See here!" He turned the printout he was holding so that she could read it, and indicated one particular section of it with a stubby forefinger.

"It's a bit too specialised for me to follow," Parvati admitted after a few seconds. "Can you spell it out in lay terms?"

"Well, you know something about the basic techniques of fractionation, separating nearly but not quite identical biological compounds so that they can be individually analysed?"

"I know it can be done, and I'd recognise the equipment for doing it, but I wouldn't care to attempt it myself."

"Don't blame you." Tai sighed again, more heavily. "On the kind of scale which we realised would be necessary here, you need the most advanced mass fractionator ever designed, a Shlovsky-Har. It's about nine feet by twelve—that's because of the long distances the compounds need to be stretched out over—but . . . Well, say you poured in a bucketful of effluent from a dyeworks, containing a gram of chlorine phthalocyanine contaminated with a thousand molecules of copper phthalocyanine. Inside half an hour it would not only deliver the dyes, and the water separately, but tell you what you'd got and how much of it. We had one. Because it was big we had *only* one. And I don't have to say what became of it, do I?"

"Aboard the *Pinta?*"

"Of course. Consequently we're having to make do with time-wasting, repetitious, unreliable alternatives."

"Looking for native sources of ascorbic acid?"

Tai hesitated. He said finally, "No. I appreciate what Abdul was trying to do when he brought up that particular red herring at the progress meeting, but he knows, I'm sure, that what I said then about natural ascorbic acid here being as rare as copper-based globin on Earth was only half the truth. The way the chemistry of life is set up on Asgard, the bug we've acquired is a maverick, on a par with the bacteria on Earth that can live in boiling sulphur springs. In the ordinary course of events it wouldn't use ascorbic acid. There wouldn't *be* any for it to use.

"What we can do, of course, is the other thing I mentioned: ingest a certain amount of the substance this bug actually prefers, which our own bodies ignore, in the hope that it will then take the line of least resistance and leave our vitamin alone. But——!" He uttered an explosive compounded of frustration and rage. "We lost our big fractionator, which would enable us to purify the stuff. We lost our Roberts synthesiser, which would enable us to go one better and tailor the native molecule so that it actually *became* ascorbic acid, the ideal solution. As things stand, we have precisely one means of converting the local raw materials in large quantities: our plants, which do the job cheerfully and what's more retain in their leaves and fruits enough of the original substance to content the bug in our bowels—so far as we can estimate."

"In that case, where's the problem?" Parvati demanded. "None of your test animals have been significantly upset by the soil-grown diet they've been eating, have they?"

"True enough. But that's not proof that we can do the same, Parvati! A human being is not a rat or even a pig, which eats substantially the same kind of diet as a man. Primate metabolism differs from other animals'— for example, we can't oxidise urea to allantoin before we excrete it. We lost our rhesus macaques with the *Pinta,* of course, so . . . Anyhow, if one compound direct from the soil manages to enter the edible portions of our crops in detectable quantities, others may be doing so in amounts too small to detect with our available equipment."

He fixed Parvati with his eyes, his expression almost belligerent.

"How have you been lately? Well?"

"I have a bruise on my leg which doesn't seem to be healing properly," she admitted. "That's indicative of scurvy, isn't it? And I found blood on my toothbrush this morning."

"Yes, I'm not surprised. But, you see, if I say go ahead and issue native-grown food at the mess, for all I know I may be poisoning the entire colony."

There was a dead pause. At length Parvati said, "You've got a choice of evils, in other words."

"Yes. To risk our energy being sapped by scurvy, or to risk something which could be considerably worse." Tai shrugged. "And I haven't got any more sensitive piece of equipment than one of our own bodies. When I mentioned the need for volunteers at the meeting, I saw you bridle—don't deny it! You control yourself marvellously, but we're old friends and you don't have a monopoly of insight into other people. Yet I don't see any alternative."

"Anything which tends to separate us into classes is potentially dangerous. Our stability is precarious in spite of our apparently good progress. We dare not let any kind of élite develop among us which isn't based squarely on superior knowledge or experience. If we were to start splitting up into brave volunteer versus cowardly shirker, or expendable test subject versus indispensable expert, we could find ourselves factionalised in next to no time." Parvati uttered the warning in a flat, emotionless tone.

"So what else are we to do?" Tai snapped. "Look, could we not avoid the risk you're worried about by drawing lots, or matching to a random number series generated by one of the computers?"

"If you feel we're that desperate . . . Well, I don't like it, but it might be better than an appeal for volunteers, I suppose." She still sounded doubtful.

"We're desperate," Tai grunted. "Mark you, I don't propose to quit yet. I have a few more ideas I can try. I have three of my best aides looking for a natural source of antibiotics which we could safely use as a food-additive, to depress the level of the bowel bacteria while we're digesting our meals. That takes time, though, and a big test layout—I've had to turn over nearly the whole of the biolab here in the ship to that single project. But if we don't have a major breakthrough inside—hmmm . . . Yes, inside two weeks, maximum—we'll be beaten anyway unless we gamble."

"I suppose this is a ridiculous question," Parvati said after a few moments' thought. "But couldn't you transfer some of our hydroponic plants to—?"

"It's a ridiculous question," Tai interrupted. "We evaluated that along with every other possibility. I take it you were going to suggest starting a batch of hydroponically-grown plants outside the ship? We're going to do that anyhow. It'll still leave a gap before the crops start to yield, and another thing we're short of is gibberellins—growth-accelerators—so we can't kick them along artificially. And the established plants, inside the ship, are already being harvested at the highest level we can risk. What we have to do is at least *treble* our intake of fruit juices, vegetable juices, citrus pulp, salad leaves and what have you, on top of our ordinary diet. Not instead of: on top of!"

Parvati shivered suddenly. She said involuntarily, "It makes my skin crawl!"

"What does?"

"I—well, I guess I've known since school that everyone carries a bunch of intestinal flora around. But I've never been consciously aware of it before. And there's something almost nauseating about the idea that there are other creatures using your body, isn't there?"

"I tell you one thing," Tai said. "If that's the way you feel, there are probably a hundred more of us who feel much, much worse."

He rose, gathered his sheaf of printouts, and headed for the elevator.

Left alone, Parvati sat immobile for a minute or more. At length she reached out to the board of the computer and punched a one-word question: *scurvy?*

The printout began before she had taken her hand away. Words and phrases jumped at her, references to the skin discoloration caused by capillary leakage, easy bruising and slow healing, swollen and painful joints, bleeding gums and loosening teeth. When she did not halt the machine at that point, it progressed from the physical symptoms to the mental, citing at length Larrey's classic observation regarding troops overcome by it who were so lethargic they paid no attention to the approach of the enemy.

At that, she violently countermanded the question, swept up the printout, and regardless of the waste it entailed—for it should have been wiped and re-used—tore it across, and again, and again, until the multiple thickness was too much for her strength and she let the pieces fall and scatter like snowflakes across the polished metal floor.

FOUR   THE MOON'S MY MISTRESS

When short I have shorn my sowce face
And swigged my hornéd barrel
In an oaken inn do I pawn my skin
As a suit of gilt apparel.
The moon's my constant mistress
And the lonely owl my marrow.
The flaming drake and the night-crow make
Me music to my sorrow.
   While there I sing, "Any food, any feeding,
   Money, drink or clothing?
   Come dame or maid, be not afraid—
   Poor Tom will injure nothing."
              —Tom o' Bedlam's Song

X

AFTER A WEEK alone, time for Dennis blended into the soft contours of a dream. He had to consult his instruments before he could tell how long he had spent on the trip. He touched at island after island, one barely distinguishable from another, and made camp beside his boat—which he could run up the beaches on its hover-ducts—on the triturated shells of diatom-like sea-creatures. Small animals with tufts of greenish antennae at both ends of their bodies sometimes scattered from the crunching of his feet; they lived in tunnels an inch below the friable surface. At high tide the rocks of the shoreline dipped beneath the water; when they returned to the air, vegetable fronds dangling from their sides glowed with colours as brilliant as a parakeet's feathers, which faded to drab as the water dripped away again and were once more renewed by the tide.

On the larger islands, carrying a back-pack of instruments and wielding a machete, he picked his way up the edges of streams, sometimes squelching in mud, sometimes going on a spongy mat of dry plant-stalks, sometimes struggling through deep layers of pebbles. From the close, mossy carpet of the "Asgard grass," the range of flora extended by way of low shrubs and bushes to the big convoluted woodplants, but there were no trees. Occasionally he saw specimens of a rare type of woodplant whose massive oblate body was supported clear of the ground on multiple roots, suggestive of a banyan, and he made a note of the location, because wood from that species was exceptionally tough and pliable.

"Flowers" existed, but were neither colourful nor

sweet-scented. There was a fertilisation process akin to pollination, which mixed the curious unfamiliar gene-equivalents and maintained variety—Yoko had shown him some examples under a microscope. Fluffy, sticky fruiting bodies dangled on flexible twigs and if they did not brush against another of their kind in the wind, they eventually dried out and wafted away like thistledown.

Among the bushes and shrubs skulked a limited number of animals, all rather small—seldom bigger than a man's palm—and all herbivorous. He had seen a few, on previous trips, gnawing at the partly decayed bodies of dead fish cast ashore on the beach, but Yoko had told him this was probably due to some local mineral deficiency, for all the species which had yet been studied also gulped up sand recently wetted with sea-water and appeared to derive diet-supplements from it.

The really vigorous life of Asgard was in the sea, not on land. On a world of islands lacking birds or flying insects, there was hardly any chance of an advanced life-form developing out of water. From the human point of view that was both good and bad. It meant that land-invaders would meet no competition to speak of, but equally it meant that sea-farming, which had become the staple source of food on Earth over the last hundred years, was impossible for at least a generation or two. They had brought no sea-creatures from Earth at all, although chemical tests by Dennis and his companions on the first visit had indicated that there were scores of useful species which could live in Asgard water. If a land-animal got out of control and ran wild, perhaps through a disaster which killed its keepers, it would be more or less limited to the island where men had established it, and would not seriously disturb the local ecological balance. Turned loose in the sea, however, where there could be no pens or sheepfolds, creatures from Earth could cause incalculable harm.

There was room for error on man's home world. Here, there was no margin at all.

On one island, while sleeping on a high boulder which stuck up from the middle of a sloping sandy beach surrounded by fifty yards of clear ground in every direction, he woke under the accusing gaze of the moon—now mercifully diminishing past its full—and found a curious little beast sitting on his chest and exploring him with its tufted antennae. Asgard's animals seemed to prefer multiple sense-organs, detecting scents, vibrations and heat and cold, which could be grown back quickly after they were damaged, to irreplaceable things like eyes and tongues.

At first startled, then amused, he tried petting it, and it responded almost like a cat, arching itself to the touch. After a few minutes, it drew in its limbs and rested immobile. Shrugging, he left it there and went back to sleep. In the morning it was gone.

Later, he woke one day at dawn to find the air full of iridescent bubbles, and jumped up in excitement, realising that the Asgard bladderwrack was fruiting. He had seen it on his first visit, but only once then and not since his return. He ran to the edge of the nearest promontory and stared across the sea. Its surface was blistered with millions of little pustules; every few minutes a convulsion went through them, and another horde detached themselves and floated up into the sky.

Yoko had explained that to him, too: during the previous night, the drifting mass of bladderwrack would have contracted its hollow fronds, forcing quantities of gas that consisted of nearly eighty per cent hydrogen into the bladders which gave it its name. When the topmost layer was full, the gas started to collect in the next, and so on, until it began to distend the tenuous

membranes connecting the bladders. These tore, and
freed the pearly bubbles he was watching.

He reached out and caught one. It rested on his palm
for a few seconds, then collapsed with a puffing noise.
There was something in human skin-secretions which
attacked its tissue.

In an hour there was nothing left except some shriv-
elled black rags of organic matter, which gave off a
foetid stench and drove him away.

There were virtually no other landmarks during his
trip, and yet he was far from bored. Isolation suited
him. After the first few days, he no longer felt bur-
dened with the need to think. His pattern of behavior
became automatic. He let the boat carry him to the next
island on the schedule, chose a camp-site, located any
visible clues he could to the area where he was expected
to search, such as changes in the colour of the ground
or remnants of ancient vulcanism, and set to work con-
tentedly enough, scrabbling among rock-screes and
probing clay-beds with his portable sonar unit.

When he did discover diamonds, after only thirteen
days of travelling and in exactly the sort of place where
the computers had told him to look, he felt disap-
pointed. He looked in puzzlement at the slightly
rounded pebbles his instruments assured him were
really diamonds, although they looked dull and uninter-
esting. One of the half-dozen or so he had picked up
was nearly the size of his little fingernail, a good gem-
quality stone, and the others were like grains of rice.

Mechanically he replaced them one by one in the
test-slot of his crystalline analyser, noted the readings,
and read them off across the table of values stamped on
the device's housing. Diamond. Unequivocally. There
was absolutely nothing he could have confused them
with.

He stretched out his time at the spot as much as he

could. Using his machete, he blazed a route from his landing-site through the vegetation by scoring the bark of woodplants. He marked the beach with arrows made of white pebbles, well above the high-tide level. All that was completely superfluous; he needed to do no more than call base at his usual time and ask them to fix his location with two of the orbiting weather satellites. Then, if necessary, any other member of the colony could come here and locate the diamond deposit in less than half an hour.

Sighing, he sat down on a rock overlooking the beach, passing the largest of his diamonds from hand to hand, and wondered about reporting his find immediately. It would only take him a day and a half to get back to base in a straight line from here, and he didn't want to go back so soon. On the other hand, his purpose accomplished, he lacked the incentive to drift on aimlessly.

Perhaps he could let it depend on who answered his evening radio call. Mostly, since he set out, he had confined himself to a couple of curt sentences indicating that he was well and continuing the search. Once or twice a garrulous person had been at the other end of the radio link: Kitty, for instance, had been in the radio room by chance after running a routine check on one of her satellites, and had kept him chatting for ten minutes. From her, he had gathered obliquely that Tai was more worried than ever about their diet, but everyone else had been emphatically cheerful, as though they didn't want him to worry while he was away from base on his own. He had no clearer idea of what had happened since his departure.

There was another hour or two to go before sunset. He peeled off his suit and spread it out on the sunward side of his boat, which he had beached as usual. He was just about to lie down and add another shade to the deep tan he had acquired, when out of memory sprang Parvati's voice, asking if he liked to swim.

He turned to stare at the water, wondering. He felt dirty and clammy, although he wasn't—he had washed down daily in fresh water, using the boat's inflatable emergency raft as a bath-tub. But that wasn't the same as going for a swim.

Am I crazy?

But even as he asked himself the question, he found he was walking towards the water. Surely just paddling around in the shallows wouldn't hurt! Yoko and her colleagues had been studying Asgard's aquatic life intensively since their arrival; they hadn't reported any danger.

The coolness was marvellous on his feet and ankles. The sand was firm, matching the best beaches of Earth. The water was clear enough for him to see anything that came his way, surely—

Abruptly he threw himself forward and struck out in a luxurious crawl, every muscle of his frame signalling pleasure at the exercise. Fifty yards from shore he trod water, shook back his wet hair, and let go a yell of pure animal delight. He porpoised up and down, surfaced, porpoised again, and rolled on his back, sighing.

Now this would be the right way to tackle Asgard! Polynesian fashion! Spending more time each day in water than on land, chasing the strange denizens of the ocean into their own—

What was that?

There had been a touch on his calf, and a momentary stinging. Alarmed, his brain ice-cold, he rolled and peered about him. Something shapeless, from which depended many reddish fronds, was darting away from him.

He put his head down, furious with himself, and

swam fast for the beach. As he scissored with his legs, he felt the area on his calf turn first very cold, then very warm, prickling with heat. The reaction spread; now it was at his hip, now beginning to affect the breathing-muscles in his belly. He gasped, glanced up to see how much further to shore, found that the shore was infinitely far away down a blue and green tunnel, scraped his knees on the bottom, and half-crawled, half-fell, the rest of the distance to his boat.

There, the universe spun, and he let go his hold on it.

XI

DISSOLVING . . .
Huge arms weak as water the hero wielded and came by the land and the sea to the western shore where the ocean of oceans reached to lap the star-sphere.

Retreating . . .
Hotcoldhotcoldhotcold: changing with every beat of his heart, now arctic, monstrous blocks of ice sterile as the daughter of a dead star, next furnace, pounding and blazing *thump* with black slag shivering off like the crust of a red iron bar under the slam of the hammer that beats the anvil.

Exploding . . .
Beside some narrow path that skirts Aldebaran and the Pleiades the cool enchanter worked, webbed, wove the coat of mail, and on each separate piece he laid a *gei*s. The manner of the *geasa* was multiplex: on this shirt one, on that gauntlet one, on that helm one, un-alike.

Decaying . . .

A hand came out of heaven with a rope, and pulled the moon down.

It lay on the ocean as it had been an egg, fair and silver, steady as a solid isle, and those came who saw and marvelled, saying, "Surely it is the fabled Tir na nOc, and those who dwell there are the Tuatha dé Danann. In that blest land is no sadness but the pleasant days of summer last yearlong. Do they crave the sweet music of harpers they but strike the air and it resounds of itself with surpassing melody; do they have lust to pleasure with a woman, such maidens come forth as were not seen in this mortal world, no, not though Deirdre herself were multiplied; do they hunger for battle and a hero's honour, then may they lock in combat all day long, and on the morrow wounded and hale, quick and dead, assemble once more together at the festive board. There mead runs on the pebbles of the streams, there fruit makes tree-boughs creak to stand the load, there one may take such jewels as he pleases to deck his garb, the diamond and the ruby, the peridot and the pearl. And should a monster or a giant from otherwhere beyond mortal ken trespass into the land and fright the folk, then call they to their aid the Ones Who Were, and in the fray the names are heard which made the very welkin sing with joy—Nuada of the Silver Hand, Finn son of Cool, and even Cú Chulainn!"

Therefore the hero mused, and spoke at last of envy, poison-deep in his heart, to go among the Blest and match his strength to Nuada Argatlam, to play at chess with Finn the son of Cool and bait Cú Chulainn till he turned around within his skin and the hairs of his head glowed red with fire and blood.

So they took great store of provision and set it on a

ship, and that ship was wide as an island and deep as an ocean gulf. In it they loaded the choicest goods and gear, into its belly they drove the royal cattle of the hero, in its great hold they laid the cauldron which he might sup from ever and not want for sustenance. He took about him the coat of mail he had, the helm he had he set upon his head, the gauntlets he had he drew over his hands that were skilled at the swordplay and the axe-play and the touch of a fair maid's bosom, the boots he put on which he had and whatever else was needful: a loom and a wheel, an awl and a needle, a hammer and a saw.

Upon him he took his *geasa* and he did not know.

For days and nights and days he sailed to the west, and to the west, and to the west, and before him always the shining land was seen. Fair the way was and pleasant, the silver pathway of the setting moon, and he sang as he sailed. Long time he supped of the never-failing cauldron, long time he ate of the cattle he had that like Manannán's pigs rose on the morrow to be slain again. Storms came, and bore his ship against the land.

Then he cried for aid and none heard him, and in rage he cursed the Tir na nOc, and the first *geis* laid upon him came to pass.

That he shall knock, and, knocking, break the door.

He hurled from him the magic cauldron that he had, and it split the silver roof of Tir na nOc as it had been an egg's shell; so gave him passage, and the second *geis*.

That he shall pass the hearth, and yet not pass.

They went from him, the magic cattle, when he drove them in, and browsed at large upon the grass of that country, and grew wise; for this was the nature of the plants which were found there, that brute beasts should learn wisdom and men should learn truth. Hungered, the hero would have passed a hearth where food was made, and the savoury smell drew him. None was nigh. He dipped his finger in the pot and tried a taste; so staunched his hunger, and the final *geis*.

That he shall eat the food and learn the truth.

Then he went forth mad, and as Sweeny ate the berries and the wild watercress, nested in the tops of trees with birds, and lay with beasts upon the naked sward. Thorns tore his flesh and made the red blood flow, harsh burrs tangled in his flowing hair, sharp pebbles cut his tender walking feet. Where he went the earth was planted with his gore. He could not speak save of the truth he learned: that men shall die, and . . .

I too am a man.

The truth grew easier to bear. The burden lightened. But to be in Tir na nOc he could not stand. He cast aside hope, care and wits, and swam back down the moonpath of the ocean. The shore he had left grew clearer, and his feet found purchase. Stepping up the beach, he turned to ash, like the friend of Bran who melted in a moment, and blew on the wind to the four wide corners of the world.

Then, in the last moment, he knew it was a *síd*, where time was altered and a day might be a thousand years. Without a mouth to shape his moans he cried the sadness and the pity of it all, and none heard.

None heard.

None heard . . .

"No word from Dennis?" Parvati whispered to Hassan as they took their places facing the colonists.

Hassan shook his head without looking at her. "I've had someone standing by the monitor all night," he muttered. "I don't like this at all, Parvati! Anything could have happened to him!"

"We'll have to send out a search party," she said.

"We know approximately where he must have been by the time he was next due to call up."

"Yes, but not immediately, I'm afraid. We must give him another day. Can I?"

"Things are bad enough without announcing that he's sick or dead," Parvati admitted. "And even if you didn't say it outright, people's imaginations are ready to invent the worst right now." She bit her lip. Dennis's unaccountable radio silence had terrified her; she could feel her own self-control wearing away like the bank of a river in spate.

"I guess it could just be that something went wrong with his communications gear," she said with forced cheerfulness, and leaned back in her chair as Hassan rose to address the meeting.

It was quite different in atmosphere from any of their previous general meetings. For one thing, it was out of schedule, in the middle of a month. For another, it was the first at which signs of disease had been perceptible. On at least half the faces arrayed before Parvati she could detect the little dark patches which indicated scurvy bruises, quick to happen, slow to heal. And not a few of the colonists had moved like old folks when they took their places, they being afflicted already with swollen, painful joints.

Worst, though, was the lethargy she could sense. No one was talking. People had barely responded to Hassan's rising. *Soldiers that took no notice of the approach of the enemy* . . .

She stifled that, and forced herself to concentrate.

"You know by now that the news is not good," Hassan said bluntly. "Tai, will you give us the details, please?"

Looking very weary, the biologist rose. His voice was quieter than usual, and several people distant from him had to strain to catch what he said.

"Yes, we're in trouble," he muttered. "Since I first announced the occurrence of scurvy among us, and explained what it was due to, we've had practically no success in developing the cures we hoped for. Meantime, the damnable bug we're all playing host to is no longer simply depleting our intake of ascorbic acid—in some of us, it's preventing our absorbing any at all. There's none left after the bug has finished.

"We tried to find a specific for the bug, which would reduce the infestation rate. We think we have one at long last—at any rate, since yesterday evening a culture of it in our biolab has been stabilised by a local antibiotic extracted from a sort of mould we found on a dead fish. We've got to find more of that mould, quickly, but even so that's not the half of the problem. Without the equipment we need to synthesise complex organics, we'll have to rely on extraction from a natural source, and we haven't even got our big fractionator, which could do the job on the scale we need.

"Still, that is a ray of hope at last. And there's another crumb of comfort for us, too. The bacteria we're carrying don't multiply indefinitely; there's a stable population level for the conditions in a human gut, and we've reached it. We won't get any worse. Or rather, the only way we'll get worse is through deprivation of ascorbic acid. If we increase our intake above the level which the bug requires, it won't bother us any further.

"The snag is still what it was before, though. The only source from which we can draw extra ascorbic acid is in the leaves and fruit of our soil-grown crops. We've not yet had any animals fall ill from eating them, which is reassuring, but I'm afraid we are going to have to have human tests before we can be sure that food is safe. Our metabolism is far more sensitive than any of our surviving equipment. Parvati, will you put my idea to the meeting, please?"

He sat down, and Parvati rose, hoping her voice would remain steady. She said, "If we're going to maintain our schedule until the winter, we need to be more vigorous than we are right now. I'm sure you can feel the bad effects of the deficiency already. I certainly can. Tai recommends, and Abdul and I agree reluctantly, that we should pick six test subjects, completely at random, in the following way." She laid her hand on a computer remote before her.

"The computers will punch out a random series of six numbers between 1 and 180. We'll toss a coin to decide whether we go through the alphabetical list of our names from the beginning or the end of the alphabet. The six names which correspond to the random numbers will be those of the test subjects. Is that a reasonable suggestion?"

She waited. She could almost see the sluggish minds of her listeners examining and discarding the alternatives: *Volunteers better, so that I can hang back? But wouldn't I feel ashamed? Then they'd have to choose among the volunteers anyway, and if I were one I'd know I could have opted to be left out, and the odds this way are thirty to one against it being me, the best I can hope for . . .*

There were nods, and not a single voice raised in dissent. Hassan spread out the list of the survivors, produced a coin—a souvenir belonging to someone, presumably, for it would be a long time before money was useful on Asgard—and tossed it for Parvati to call.

"Heads at the beginning!" she said. It fell tails, and Hassan punched the computer remote. In less than a second the numbers rattled out, and in a dry voice he began to recite the names.

"Tai Men. Dan Sakky."

She saw the big African's face fall, unashamedly, but

a moment later he gave a shrug and leaned back in his seat.

"Kitty Minakis. Abdul Hassan."

Is that damned computer plotting against us? It's naming key personnel, section chiefs, not aides! And Abdul himself! Preserve us, preserve us!

"Parvati Chandra. Ulla Berzelius. And that's the six." Hassan folded the list and resumed his seat.

"Me?" Parvati said to him faintly.

He nodded, maintaining his outward calm but failing to prevent a tremor in his voice when he answered, "Yes, you, Parvati. And me."

XII

IT WAS AS though he found his body again piecemeal: his left hand being thrust into the burrow of some sand-living creature, to be withdrawn with a moue and a grunt of disgust; the hollow drum of his belly as it gave back *something* turned to a foul slimy liquid; his eyes separately but both as hot prickling globes, jamming in their orbits on the friction of intangible sand; the dry tube that formerly had been a mouth and throat, inhabited by a fearful independent worm that he had to take between finger and thumb before he could recognise it as a tongue.

But there were gaps. Nothing from wrist to shoulder, nothing from hip to knee.

Until, completely without warning, like the implosion of a galaxy, he reassembled from all the scattered directions in which he had been hurled and was—*here.*

Surrounded by diamonds!

He gazed uncomprehending at the torrent of sparkling gems that passed before his eyes, and began to count his heart-beats to see how long they would go on flowing. The idea of diamonds gave way little by little, and he was able to conceive of them being something else.

Bits of sunlight broken up on water.

He was squatting cross-legged over his hips in a narrow stream, cool from the waist down, but his back and shoulders hot with the sun. He had a vague memory of thirst, but when he attended to the condition of his mouth, to see if it was dry, he discovered it was fresh and moist, and there was a coolness inside him as well as outside.

I've been drinking unpurified water!

From wherever it had been driven, his power of judgment returned, and on the instant he wished it had not. Appalled, he leapt to his feet, almost losing his balance as a large round pebble turned under his weight, and stared down at his body. On his calf, where he had brushed against the water-creature while swimming, there was a fading reddish patch traversed by three parallel dotted lines of scabs. Reflexively he touched them with his fingertips as though to scratch an intolerable itch, and found exact correspondence.

That apart, however, to his amazement he felt well. Here and there he had grazed or cut himself; there was one cut in particular, under the arch of his right foot, which was tender and made him limp a trifle, but like all the other wounds it was perfectly clean and healing normally. His left shoulder ached very slightly, from a mending sprain, he concluded. It was past the stage of inconveniencing him. He swung the arm experimentally to prove it.

Damnation, though . . . Oughtn't I to be dead?
Well—maybe I am!

The two ideas surfaced simultaneously in his mind: one rational, due to awareness of the fearful risks he must have run while deprived of reason, the other plainly absurd yet carrying an aura of truth because somewhere in the vague, dream-like memories he could recall a similar notion had appeared to make excellent sense.

Absently he reached up to his nape, and gave a start. His hair had grown noticeably.

How long have I been . . . away?

He stared about him, looking for landmarks, and spotted one of the blazes he had cut on the track connecting the diamond deposit with the beach on which he had left his boat. With great concentration, trying to prevent himself from panicking, he picked his way in the indicated direction. A few minutes, and he was in sight of the beach where he had enjoyed his brief and calamitous bathe.

The boat was still there, unharmed, although a great many small creatures had invaded it: a glutinous mess of egg-cases adhered to the instrument board, which he had to scrape clean with a stick before he could read the dials.

Ten days!

What must they be thinking, back at the base island? Were they wasting precious time and energy on hunting him? But that didn't make sense. They had a record of his search-pattern, and he had called in as usual the night before he found the diamonds, so they would have been able to locate him within a hundred miles or so—they should have found him and carried him back to the *Santa Maria*'s sick-bay within at most three days.

Why hadn't they done so?

Beginning to be really frightened now, he turned to the radio and hit the call switch. Nothing happened. Yet he knew there was a monitor permanently on his frequency; he should at once have heard the high sweet hum of the emergency recorder. Briefly puzzled, he

gazed blankly at the set. Abruptly he realised what
might have happened, unclipped the front panel, and
saw with a sinking heart that one of the native fauna
had settled here, too. A creature five or six inches long,
armed with erosive limbs hooked like a snail's rasping
tongue, had cleared itself a vacant spot in the heart of
the mechanism.

He seized it and hurled it towards the sea in a burst
of futile fury. Calming almost at once, he turned to look
for his suit, discovered it partly hidden by wind-drifted
sand, shook all the tunnelling creatures out of it and
made sure his sealed gun and medikit were undamaged.
From the latter he extracted a diagnostic chew and
placed it in his mouth. He counted for the requisite
thirty seconds, his jaw going mechanically, then withdrew it and placed it in the appropriate slot on the lid
of the kit.

After a further half-minute, there was a click and the
dial reported that he was apparently in good health,
with one qualification. But the portable device wasn't
sensitive enough to tell him what that was.

Somewhat cheered, because the clean diagnosis implied that whatever else might have happened during
his fit of insanity the principle that Earthly creatures
didn't pick up Asgard diseases still held good, he piled
the kit, suit, and gun on the passenger seat of the boat
and scrambled into the pilot seat himself. Gingerly, because if that animal had wrecked the radio one of its
cousins might have ruined another and more essential
piece of equipment, he checked the drive. The engine
emitted a normal throbbing drone, and all the instruments read as they should.

He was on the point of feeding power to the drive
and heading for base, when he halted his hand an inch
from the main control lever.

Food?

He twisted around in the seat and stared over his shoulder at the rack of cartoned meals within arm's reach. They looked as he remembered, and as they should have looked, after he had drawn thirteen days' allowance. One carton had suffered the attentions of a local animal, and its corner was torn, but the thief had clearly found the contents inedible and left them alone after a few bites.

I ought to be hungry.

He switched off the power and sat shivering as a vivid, revolting memory came clear in his mind. He had vomited, and spewed a great gout of liquid all over himself. What had been in him, that his stomach rejected so violently? And more alarming still: what was in him now, that he did not feel hungry despite not touching his packaged stores for ten mortal days . . . ?

He closed his eyes for a moment, for the world was tilting dizzily. He clutched the reassuring hardness of the control lever until his thinking calmed and he was able to face the important point that if he had managed to live by eating Asgard foodstuffs he must try and work out what they were. So far as he knew, Tai Men had not even begun a programme to determine whether native plants were nutritious. Possibly he had even chanced—blindly, crazily—across a key to the scurvy problem which had still been plaguing the colony the last time he spoke on the radio.

He wanted desperately to head for the base island to see another human face, hear a voice and lie under a roof again. But he steeled himself against the impulse to leave right away. He gathered a camera and a biological sampling kit, and got out of the boat.

For the best part of three hours he trudged back and forth around the island, trying to reconstruct his movements. He took a sample of water from the stream in which he had found himself when he recovered. Clearly, he had drunk from it without purifying it, and was none the worse. That was significant. So, too, were the gnaw-marks he spotted on the cabbagy stem of one of the shrubs, that at first he mistook for a blaze he had cut to show the trail. But those were the traces of teeth, not a machete.

He collected samples of his own excrement, which he had dropped like an animal wherever the need overtook him, and sealed them in airtight bags. They were unat-tacked by the native scavengers—one of the reasons why sewage disposal was likely to become a major problem on Asgard, requiring all-chemical treatment without aid from bacteria—and he saw in them shreds of tough bark-like material, small round objects resem-bling tomato-pips, and other substances that had appar-ently gone through his bowel unaltered. Yet he had in-contestably been nourished by his improbable diet. He was fit and strong, as though he had been under the supervision of an expert dietitian.

Shaking his head, he returned to the boat with his load of samples. Having stowed them, he turned on the power for the second time, eased his craft up on its hoverducts, and set the automatics to take him back to base at maximum speed, regardless of wasted power.

During the terrible day and a half of suspense which he had to endure while the boat carried him along, he struggled to make sense out of the experience he had undergone. The ten missing days of his life were not wholly blank, though that would have been alarming enough. What frightened him was that most of the memories, elusive as dreams, which he could recapture didn't match the objective traces of his activities that he had found when he went back to collect those samples.

He had walked and lain down, slept and eaten—that much was clear. But the few rational-seeming images he could recover to correspond with his deductions, such such as the one of vomiting, were embedded in a matrix of confusion. He could tell that something had happened which must in its way be as pregnant with unspeakable meaning as the fit of madness that caused him to throw Sigrid down naked on an alien beach. But his conscious awareness seemed to have been disconnected. Fragments of legend came to him, isolated, in response to the mental clues which had always before conjured up sane memories, as though his experience had been so fearful he was compelled to interpret it to himself in parables drawn from the ancient lore in which he had been steeped at home on Earth: tales of the great heroes like Finn and Cú Chulainn.

Had he now, again, collapsed under the pressure of a strange world? To use the comparison he had employed when talking to Parvati, had Asgard sprung another trap for him? Or was there some physical cause, perhaps some poison which the sea-beast had injected into his bloodstream?

It was useless to try and guess, he decided. He was going to have to wait until Tai and Parvati could take him apart for inspection.

It was in the cool pale light of dawn that he woke from uneasy slumber, dogged by random pictures from his weird experience, to find he was in sight of the base island and the automatics were buzzing to alert him. He knuckled his eyes and peered through the morning twilight.

Starting, he realised something was wrong. His boat was lying to off the south of the small harbour, and it was unchanged. But by now Dan Sakky's boat-sheds should have been completed. The whole aspect of the harbour should have changed. But there was nothing new—correction: there was only a line of foundations, with nothing on them.

And beyond, up the hill towards the *Santa Maria*, things were subtly amiss. A solar collector had been knocked down and lay draped over a woodplant, randomly. Someone had decorated a power-line with knotted rags, like the paper shreds on the tail of a kite.

He rose in the boat as it bore him into the harbour, a great shadow of fear overcoming him, and called out loudly. From a hiding-place among rocks a figure rose, levelling a gun, and he recognised Saul Carpender.

"Saul! It's me—Dennis!" he cried. "What's wrong? Something is wrong, isn't it?"

Unshaven, red-eyed, marked with scurvy bruises, Saul peered down at him as though struggling to convince himself that the new arrival was indeed a friend. Eventually he lowered the gun and rubbed his bristly chin with the back of his hand.

"Oh, it's you," he muttered. "More or less given you up for lost, I guess . . . Well, come ashore, and help us sort out the mess we're in, hm? Abdul's gone crazy, and Parvati, and Dan and Tai and Ulla and Kitty—mad as hatters, the lot of them!"

FIVE   WAKING SOULS

The palsy plague these pounces
When I prig your pigs or pullen,
Your culvers take, or mateless make
Your Chanticleer, and sullen.
When I want provant with Humphrey
I sup, and when benighted
To repose in Paul's with waking souls
I never am affrighted.
    But still do I sing, "Any food, any feeding,
    Money, drink or clothing?
    Come dame or maid, be not afraid—
    Poor Tom will injure nothing."
                    —Tom o' Bedlam's Song

XIII

WAITING FOR THE moment of truth to come upon her, Parvati was nervous: felt her palms moist, her belly taut with apprehension. Yet the anxiety was impersonal. It had little to do with the idea that she might be due to swallow a poisoned draught, though intellectually she was calculating with that possibility. What disturbed her far more deeply was that if the computers had been deliberately trying to sabotage the colony, they could hardly have picked a less expendable group of test subjects.

Kitty we could manage without; most of her work is done. And, without being slighting, Dan Sakky too. We could cobble makeshifts together without Dan's capacity for visualising unbuilt structures, though it would take longer and lead to great waste of effort. But how could we manage without Ulla to lead us to mineral deposits like a diviner sensing water, or Tai to watch our first babies from embryo to delivery, or Abdul to ride our fractious team, resentful of harness, or—or me?

Should the crucial event have been a solemn affair, watched over by the entire band of colonists? The possibility only occurred to her when the test group had assembled in the biolab of the *Santa Maria,* among racked experimental tanks and creeper-like festoons of translucent plastic piping along which bubbled noisy nutrient solutions. It was due to the remarkable ordinariness of the circumstances.

With astonishment she realised: *I never consciously risked my life and health before! Even when I stepped out on the surface of Asgard for the first time, I knew that it had been proved superficially safe by the first vis-*

itors. How did Dennis feel, the first to take an unfiltered breath of Asgard air?

But she couldn't ask him. He wasn't here, and no one knew what had become of him except that he must be at a place they could locate on a map, tomorrow at latest, and go to in search of him.

Meantime, she had this obscure annoying feeling that there should be a kind of ceremony to mark this commitment she was making. Life was a precious and irreplaceable possession. If she was going to gamble it, ought there not to be some special ritual to mark the moment forever?

She kept that to herself, however, for when she glanced at her companions she found they were all—at least outwardly—composed. They were tense, like her, but what betrayed the fact was no more than, for example, Kitty's uncharacteristic silence, a frown on Dan's broad ebony brow.

For better or worse, it was going to be a very unremarkable occurrence, this test on which the future of the Asgard colony might depend. They had all been here scores of times, in exactly similar surroundings, during the first month after landing. Then, Tai had conducted daily tests on members of the group, studying water and stool samples, blood and serum samples, nail-parings, hair-clippings, reflexes, everything which might indicate danger to their health. During the outbreak of acute diarrhoea which had afflicted them all, without exception, for up to a week, she had been left with the impression that this biolab was the centre of the whole venture, but that scare had proved groundless and they had adjusted happily to their alien intestinal flora.

Or so we all thought . . .

But everything was so familiar and ordinary! Under Tai's directions, a couple of his aides were dropping round golden oranges into a conventional juice-extractor, leaves of spinach and spikes of red carrot into a big blender from the kitchens, adding sugar to one and salt to the other, for palatability! It seemed absurd!

Even the unaccustomed presence of Tibor Gyorgy, overseeing the medical test equipment in his capacity as their chief electronicist, wasn't enough to provide the symbolism she wanted, which would have made her feel she was really committing herself. She was going to go through it without involvement, detached, distant from reality.

And there, now, was Tai himself raising a glass of the first juice to emerge from the extractor and gulping it down. Saying, "Tastes okay, that's for sure! Right, mark the precise time down, will you? Urine tests at one hour and three hours, blood tests at one, two and four, absolutely without fail. I'll have my stomach pumped after the next batch, but there's no need to inflict that on everybody. Who's next—you, Parvati? Fruit or vegetable juice?"

And she heard herself choose the latter, and could tell no difference as the cool dark fluid slipped past her teeth and into the darkness without recall of her mysterious metabolism.

Exactly what everyone had expected to see by way of result, she couldn't tell. It was clear from the covert glances her companions who had not sampled the native-grown juices gave whenever they thought she wouldn't notice that they were unconsciously looking for some outward clue to what had happened. Outward or inward, she could detect none herself, except that by the second day of the trial she seemed to have lost a grey depression so subtle she had barely been aware that she was suffering from it—the penumbra of scurvy, presumably. She deliberately pinched a generous fold of her forearm as hard as she could between finger and thumb, and looked again after half an hour. There was no trace of the darkening which would follow the rupture of scurvy-weakened capillaries.

We're going to make it, she decided with premature optimism. And, as she went on her rounds of the base island, saw nothing to convince her otherwise. All the test subjects were as fit as she was, so far, and that meant a trifle fitter than many of their companions. Her duties took her to every corner of their microcosm of mankind's world at least once every day, and as she went from the kilns where they were firing their own clay dishes to the miniature furnace that produced steel reinforcement rods for Dan, from the sawmill stacking up its supplies of planks to the scrap-reclaiming team denuding the *Niña*, she noted everywhere the insidious lethargy and barely-controlled irritability which Tai had warned against.

There was one additional problem, however, which remained in the forefront of her mind. What about Dennis Malone?

The evening when he had failed to call in, for the first time this trip though not the first time ever, she had begun to worry, but on his last trip he had, admittedly, missed one call and reported in on schedule the next day, not bothering to apologise. According to Ulla, moreover, by now he should be in the most promising of all the suspected locations where diamonds might be found. It was entirely possible he had wandered a long distance from his boat and the radio in it, been overtaken by nightfall close to a site he wanted to investigate by daylight, and decided to camp where he was.

When he failed to call in the next day as well, she grew really alarmed, but by then the need to undergo all Tai's metabolic tests—a total of eighteen of them in every twenty-four hour period—and the demands of her routine work which must be kept up at all costs conspired to make her and Abdul put off the dispatch of a search-party until the day following, although they were both agreed on the importance of it. It took time to select a group who could be spared, too. But in the end one of Ulla's aides, one of Dan's, and Yoko, were chosen and briefed. The colony's second-line cushion-foil was checked out by Saul, stocked for the trip, which would be short because it would only need to include a straight-line leg out and back, and programmed appropriately.

So, first thing in the morning, the rescue party would set off. And would find . . .

Restless, she lay on her bunk and listened to the sounds of their village settling down for the night: doors closing, people calling good night to one another, the crunching noise of footsteps as the two colonists on overnight watch in the ship went up to relieve the evening pair. Two people were always stationed aboard the *Santa Maria* from sunset to midnight and midnight to dawn, on guard against the emergency which had not materialised.

The nights were still warm well into the small hours, although the first hints of fall could be detected now. A revised wind-forecast had caused Kitty to ask Dan to attend to the securing of the houses with guys before, instead of after, building his boat-sheds, and that encouraged a tremor of apprehension. But in general things were going well, as before. Certainly she and the other five test subjects were showing only good effects from their trial diet-additives.

She tossed and turned, inexplicably unable to relax and sleep though she was feeling healthily tired after another long day. Saul had asked if he could join her for the night, but Tai had suggested that none of the test subjects kiss anyone until the results were all in— transfer of saliva was potentially liable to skew his in-

strument readings. Was that why she was so restless?
She liked Saul well; his dry personality appealed to her,
perhaps because his background made him more at
home than most of the colonists on this world of widely
scattered islands. Being used to an environment resem-
bling this, he was relaxed.

Lying on her back, gazing up at the exposed ceiling-
joists and overlapping shingles of her room—the kind
of thing she had never seen at home on Earth, which no
one saw to pay attention to unless like Dan they were
involved in the actual construction of a building before
the finish was fitted to it—she began to wonder absently why the planners of the Asgard colony had been
so insistent on complex, relatively inefficient designs
like this, with its flat roof and four-square layout.
Granted, the right angle was an intellectual achieve-
ment, symbolising man's intervention. But would it not
have been better to employ, say, Dymaxion domes,
which could equally have been built from local materials and afforded them greater privacy, better insulation
during the coming winter, more space to move around
in for a given quantity of effort?

Yes, certainly that roof should be domed. She bulged
it upward in her imagination, and it receded from her.
Passive, she watched it balloon out, noting also: *I feel
very giddy.*

Indeed, suddenly her head was swimming. The roof
came down again, rose, came down, like the pulsing of
a vast heart. Its latest descent threatened to crush her.
Alarmed, she rolled off the bunk and crouched on the
floor, on hands and knees, gazing upwards with her
mouth ajar.

Something's happening to me. What—?

She clawed to her feet, clutching the edge of the
bunk. The floor rose and fell under her like a stormy
sea. Uttering a faint moan, she put one foot before the

other until she reached the door and was able to fumble it open. Across the threshold: the sights and sounds and smells of an alien world.

The thought of death became real to her, and she tried to run from it, quite naked, into the alien night.

XIV

MAY THE GOD *Soma, he who is called the moon, liberate me!*

Charnel-house moon, the abode of the dead, where crushed corpses lie intermingled with shattered fragments of metal, plastic, glass, ceramic, bone . . .

Indra is Svargapati: see the dome of heaven, lit with the jewels that flowed from the mouth of Bali whom he slew. Those that were his bones are diamonds and his marrow emeralds; from his blood sprang rubies, drop by drop; his teeth were pearls, his blue eyes shattered into sapphires beyond the power of man to count, his very flesh turned translucent as crystal. Indra is Megha-vahana, and the clouds pile in the west, ready steeds for his riding. Indra is Vajri, thunderer.

And the storms will come.

May the god Soma, he who is called the moon, give me release!

The first to die: Yama, king of the dead, lord of the reservoir of oblivion. Garlanded with skulls, the stems of lilies threaded through the empty sockets of their eyes, his mouth a mockery of a human smile—that great gaping grin, wide as a gate, through which all men created take their way . . .

The instant of Agni: the striking of fire. "First cut the wood of the Sami tree, then make a wand with the wood of the tree Asvattha. By turning one against the other you will make fire." Thus the Gandharvas. This done, the creation of Agni, who was cursed to eat all things for telling the truth.

May the god Soma, he who is called the moon, make me free!

Pledged that he would not attack with weapons of wood or stone or iron, nor with anything wet or dry, neither by day nor by night, Indra yet struck down the demon Vritra. Vishnu incarnate in a cloud of foam was his club, at the moment when the sun cut the horizon. Thus he turned preservation to destruction. Ponder this, O Born of Woman, and learn that all things are one.

Filled with divine fury, Mother Kali struck down her husband, trampled him in the midst of the heaping corpses. By this she was made ashamed, but nothing changed. The mother that gives birth shall also inevitably destroy; Vishnu the preserver shall be made a killing tool; the moon that is the holy cup of soma shall be drained, and Kali-Durga shall reign, and Yama, in the age of Shiva, who destroys all things. For all things are *maya*. The wheel turns. In every dimensionless point of the universe there may be found an Enlightened One.

Helpless with wonderment under the failing moon, Parvati Chandra looked at herself. She touched her breasts and made to strike a gash across one's underside, covering the other, because it seemed somehow wrong to know that there were two. "Durga, my sister," she murmured, and wondered about the death which must come forth from her womb. Blood ran down dark from the tip of the finger whose sharp nail she had used to mark herself.

Also . . .

The giddiness overtook Tai Men while he was asleep, so that his trained awareness fought a losing battle all the way up the shivering tunnels from unconsciousness towards the peak of wakefulness. At one point knowledge and experience were precisely poised, but he was not yet in command of his faculties; he could know, but he could not act. When he was able to, the action he took was merely to stagger from his bunk, through the door of his room, and out under the palace floor of the August Personage of Jade.

The Heavenly Master of the First Origin was long gone to his deserved retirement, leaving to fend as best they could those awkward, clumping creatures whom his successor had made from clay and carelessly left in the rain, so that when the breath of life was wished on them, some went halt, some were blind, some ugly and deformed. This was a matter for which there would be a calling to account at the end of the divine year; meantime, from an infinite distance, the Celestial Master of the Dawn of Jade of the Golden Door looked on benevolently, wishing them well in their brief span before the inception of his reign.

Beyond that he had no interest in them. They might do as they chose.

To the moon, as it is prescribed, on the fifteenth day of the eighth month: a sacrifice in the form of fruit. Perhaps this is what the Divine Hare takes, there in the palace of the moon, and makes with it the elixir of immortality. Yet to live long without wisdom does not mean happiness. Witness the discomfiture of I, the Excellent Archer, who once saved the world in the very long ago, whose wife the most beautiful of all created women is under the protection of the Hare, the patron of those men who will have no commerce with women. He had the elixir first, for his shooting of the nine fierce suns that threatened to burn the world, and by it lost his wife.

Thirty and three are the levels of Heaven. One may ascend by virtue and aspire to be a god oneself, but to become a god is not assurance of eternal bliss. There is a reckoning. There is a calling to account.

Do not fail. The laws are strict. There is no celestial compunction about dismissing those who prove inadequate. There is only the benign authority of the August Personage of Jade, who gives and takes impartially according to what you have deserved.

The Second Lord may come upon you in any of two and seventy guises, eager in the business of his emperor. His dog may rend you like an evil spirit. Do what you must without resentment; that way freedom lies, and no fear.

In the palace of the moon resides the most beautiful of women, Chang-O who was once the Excellent Archer's wife. It is not reported that she and her husband had children. She sits and drinks the elixir of immortality with the Hare. It is improbable that her new protector will father children on her. It is said, discreetly behind lacquered screens in cool halls of marble where such important subjects may fitly be discussed, that the

Hare has no urge in that direction. It is said that this is
why men take no part in the sacrifice of the autumn
equinox, of fruit to the full moon. They are afraid for
their virility. They will not risk the certainty of dutiful
children against the hypothesis of everlasting life.

Tai Men, who had made the sacrifice of fruit under
the moon, sat weeping on a rock beside the road, and
could not be consoled for the loss he had not suspected
before it was too late.

Also . . .

In sleep where he was building beautiful imaginary
cities, organically conceived like the densest natural
jungle, yet substantial and efficient like a single vast
machine, there was Daniel Sakky, the big dark man
whose thews and muscles made it seem he could himself have heaped up the high towers of which he
dreamed, instead of tracing them in delicate shadowy
forms on the input board of a computer and leaving
quiet metal machines to give them solidity.

Still three-quarters immersed in his visions, he wandered out across the raw new ground of Asgard, at first
puzzled, growing little by little more afraid.

Masks of straw and wood daubed with coloured mud
lending them a repellent, awe-inspiring aspect, the old
wise men sat and explained the universe. Under the
thatched roof of the hut no outsider might enter on pain
of magic sickness, the drums spoke with a supernatural
voice. On that spear the blood of a leopard not yet dry,
glistening in the wan flame of a mystic fire; the skin of
the beast shrouding the spindly limbs of the oldest and
wisest of all them who spoke, to symbolise what naked
weakling man could do by power of thought and magic.

But the voices uttered warnings against arrogance.

Once the people wanted to know, "What is the moon?" And one said, "We shall climb to it and see." He took a pole and a pole and a pole, and lashed one to another and sank them in a pit in the ground. Then he took a pole and a pole and a pole and climbed to secure the new ones to the first ones. After him came others, curious, eager, inquisitive. Pole after pole tied with bands of creeper, leather thongs from the hide of the hippopotamus, braided plaits of hair from the mane of a lion, very strong, very potent magic. They climbed and they climbed and still they were not at the moon, and one day the poles broke and they were all hurled to the ground and many were killed. So they never did know what the moon was, and many wives wept.

A wrinkled hand fumbled in a medicine-bag and sprinkled ghost-herbs on the fire. Inhaled, the smoke of them brought visions.

Men die, but the people of the moon do not. Why not? It will be told. Once Libanza called all to come before him, he the very powerful, the sorcerer above heaven whose hearth-smoke is the stormcloud, whose speaking drum utters the thunder when he beats it, whose knife flashes the lightning as he turns it this way and that. He said, "Come! Be quick! Attend me!"

At once the people of the moon came, running, and Libanza was pleased. But the people of the earth came walking, slowly, complaining to one another, and Libanza was angry. He said to the people of the moon, "You shall not die! You shall rest two days a month, and no more." He said to the people of the earth, "You shall rest every day, and you shall die forever, knowing because you have seen that the people of the moon only rest and rise again after two days."

* * *

Breathe deep the smoke that clogs the space below the roof. Marvels and mysteries shall be made plain: truth about life, truth about death.

By the rivers and on the forest paths, there you shall meet *Mokadi;* in the high places of the hills when you grow giddy with the thinness of the air, you shall know the spirits of the ancestors are by. In all the places where your forefathers have trod, there they are dead and there they are buried. Sometimes they are angry, for it is hard to be a ghost. But propitiate them, make offerings, play music and dance to give them pleasure, for it was they who bought you this, clear ground, fat herds, much game to wet your spear. Thanks to them you sleep with your wives and children under a good sound roof, you wear a gown of many-coloured cloth and when it is a festival day you drink much palm-wine until you laugh and laugh.

Remember those who became ghosts that we might build this village.

The voices died. The smoke blew away through the chinks under the eaves. The hands of the drummer ceased, and the blood of the leopard was dry.

Heir to all this, Daniel Sakky composed himself cross-legged at the brink of the stream, where there was heavy dull clay in quantities, and set himself to forming figures of men and women as though he, like Massim-Biambe, could inject into their substance *tchi*. He bowed sometimes to the devil-mask of the moon, for that too had been bought for him by those who turned to ghosts.

XV

Dreams as from the penumbra of the *Ragna Rökkr*, that night from which the gods themselves shall not awake, troubled the sleep of Ulla Berzelius. Her lithe tanned limbs sprawled to the four corners of her bunk, a thick tress of fair hair wound over her mouth and trailing across her breast, she dreamed of strangulation and woke to see, through the window, the moon three parts gone in the jaws of Fenris Wolf.

> *Hart es i heimi, hordomr mikkil,*
> *Skeggi-aold, skalm-aold, skildir klofnir,*
> *Vind-aold, varg-aold, adhr vaerold steipisk!*

In the day when evil dreams shall come to trouble the sleep of the Aesir, it shall go hard with Earth:

> *Hard in the home then, whoredom abounding,*
> *Sword-age, axe-age, shields are cloven,*
> *Wind-age, wolf-age, ere the world perish!*

All the cunning amassed by Father Odin, wisest of the Aesir, was of no avail. The black crows Huginn and Munin, thought and memory, brought him news of all that passed in all the worlds: Niflheim, Muspelheim, Jotunheim, Utgard, Midgard, Asgard . . . At the price of an eye he bought the secrets of Mimir, sitting by his well under the middle root of Yggdrasil, and at Mimir's death he conjured the giant's head to make it speak to him still, and answer all his questions.

It was to no avail.

Austr byr in aldnar i Iarnvidhi
Ok foedhir thar Fenris kindir.
Verdhr af theim aollom einar nokkar
Tungls tiugari, i trollz hami!

By subtlety he stole the blood of Kvasir from the giant Suttung, which the dwarfs had mingled with honey and placed in the cauldron Odrerir. Whoever drank of it should be a bard and a skald, should understand and speak of all things to the delight and wonder of the worlds. So fierce was the chase as he fled in the guise of an eagle that Suttung's heart burst asunder, following him.

No more, however, did that theft avail.

East-by in Ironwood watches the old witch
And feeds there the Fenris brood.
One of them shall be born
Formed as a fiend who shall fling down the
moon!

Nine days, nine nights, wounded with his own spear, Odin hung on the trunk of Yggdrasil and none came in to answer to his calls. Starving and clemmed with thirst, on the ninth day he saw runes on the ground, and read them aloud, and was made whole and young.

But no more did that free him from the destiny of death.

As much fascinated as terrified, Ulla walked across the island, heedless of where her feet were carrying her, her eyes fixed on the moon as it slipped into the maw of the wolf.

Likewise . . .

Head spinning like a centrifuge, Kitty Minakis drew in her small arms and legs tightly against her body, eyes wide and staring into nowhere. A form of knowledge was upon her; she needed to rise and share it, it being far too huge for a single mind to encompass. Trembling, she set out and found no one. Alone, in dark, on this small knob of ground enclosed by the illimitable waters.

Girdled by rivers—Acheron, Cocytus, Phlegethon, Lethe, Styx—it was a dark country, full of ill boding. There no apples grew, but gloomy black poplars, and willows which never bore fruit. There the ground was carpeted with asphodel, the plant of ruined cemeteries, long forgotten by the children of those who had been interred. There only the wan light of the moon was to be seen, and no birds sang.

There in the Grove of Persephone the many-headed dog Cerberus came fawning, to lick the feet of the new arrivals, wagging his horrid tail. But let him once get the scent of death from a passer-by, and from then on for ever that person should not pass again. Seeing the fearful hound who blocked the way back to the sweets and delights of Earth, the dead drank gladly of the waters of Lethe, and forgot.

There was a charge to enter the other world. It must under all circumstances be paid. Had you no obolus to pay the ferry-fee, old ferryman Charon would spit on and revile you, and take his boat off from the shore, poling with heaves and grunts, to cross the river Acheron. Abandoned, hopeless, you must mourn and roam continually on the river bank, halfway between somewhere and nowhere, until the end of time.

He who reigns over that dark country Tartarus is called Ploutos, "the rich," for of the increase in his wealth there is no end. Speak not of the forgotten treasure hidden in the earth, which he comes invisibly to steal away; speak rather of the number of his subjects, to which day by day and without ceasing there are added scores, thousands, millions!

Such is his power that every night he sends forth his agent Hypnos, whom men know as sleep, and he shows them a foretaste of the fate in store. This my Lord is the king from whom you shall not escape; sooner or later it will not be gentle Hypnos, reluctant to lay fetters on the human mind and yielding with a sigh to the advent of the pleasant nymph Aurora when she brings the dawn, but Thanatos who comes, Death who lays hard hands on the unwilling and drags them screaming and howling to the Underworld.

Where will the ferry bear us? To the dreary groves of Tartarus, there where the asphodel glimmers like the phosphorescence of rotting fish, the sweetest light that we shall ever see again, or the fields of Elysium, from whose white graceful poplars Heracles made his crown of triumph when he vanquished Cerberus? Not knowing, let us gladly drink of Lethe, that we shall forget all reason to complain of the fate we must endure. Let no one say: I pine here in Tartarus, and should be there, for I was not evil in my life on Earth. Let all forget.

Let all forget . . .

Passive, on sighting the ferry of Charon, Kitty Minakis sat down on a rock to await the arrival of the boatman who would claim her fare. She had drunk dutifully of the Lethe water. All past vain hope was gone from her.

Likewise . . .

Abdul Hassan was thankful for the quirk of heredity which made him able to survive on far less than the average amount of sleep. Five hours, sometimes six, had sufficed him on Earth. Here where the days were thirty hours long he took six more often than at home, but midnight usually found him, as tonight, sitting alone and contemplating the problems he must solve, while everyone else except the two on watch in the *Santa Maria* slept and dreamed.

But he was tired in ways which sleep could not relieve. Somewhere adrift on the face of Asgard, there was their unfortunate explorer Dennis Malone, who should have been looking forward to returning home next spring, and instead was trapped here. As though he had accepted the bread and water of Ament, The Westerner, and become the friend of the gods.

Abdul tensed. The chair he was sitting on had suddenly begun to sway, as though it were being rocked on a gentle swell. The walls enclosing him appeared to open out. Turning to face the door, which he had left ajar for the sake of the cool breeze, he saw a kind of hallway beyond. In the same instant the midnight curfew overtook him, and his light went out.

From the last course of his thoughts before this curious event set in, he retained a self-directed question: *How shall I be judged?* For it was by him, the pivot of their venture, that the success or failure of the Asgard colony hung.

Great weariness overcame him, a sense that it was now too late to make any further amends for whatever errors he had committed. Calmly he rose and went forth to face the verdict.

They waited for him in the Hall of Double Justice, and he saw them when he rose from kissing the threshold of that most sacred place. He had crossed the land between the world of the living and the world of the dead. Arrived, he had no hope of going back. What must be, must be. Let it therefore be.

At the edge of hearing he seemed to sense the mocking laughter of the lady of the West, whose bread he had eaten and whose water he had drunk. He remembered her high plume of feathers, symbol of the land of sunset. But her task was done. Invited—lured—however one should phrase it, the fact stood: he was in the Hall.

There stood a monstrous scale under the painted roof: the scale of justice, in one pan of which hung down the heart befouled with all the supplicant's sins. It tilted steeply, for the load was heavy, and that pan scraped the gaudy floor.

Beside it stood Maat the goddess of truth and justice, terrible in aspect, with eyes that could pierce any veil of dissembling the new-dead tried to screen his failings with. There too was Amemait, the devourer, the greedy beast formed of crocodile and hippopotamus and lion, eager to snatch men's souls and gobble them. Whining a little, drooling on the tiles, he fixed the supplicant with his horrid gaze.

Under a *naos*, the Lord Osiris himself, the righteous judge. On his head the *atef* flanked by ostrich feathers, arms crossed soberly upon his breast; in one hand the whip, in the other the crook, emblems of supreme power. Wound about his body, below the face tinged with the suggestive green of putrefaction—for he too died, was cut apart, was scattered to the corners of the kingdom—the winding-sheets of the dead. But his arms are free. There is hope and yet there is no hope. Oblivion is not inevitable, but what is done is done.

On either side, two and forty judges, each with a sharp-edged sword. Call each by name, and they will give a bow, but do not think to bribe them. These have gone past corruption, into incorruptibility.

There is ceremonial music: chanted prayers, the jangling of sistra. There is the scent of precious wood, burned on sacred fires to sweeten the air for the nostrils of the judges. But there is one thing more than this show and pomp. There is a man brought to the tribunal to be judged.

The pans of the scales must be balanced by the feather of truth.

Beyond hope or anxiety, beyond alarm or disquiet, Abdul Hassan waited quietly for Anubis the jackal-headed god to place the feather in the scale and see which way it tipped with its monstrous burden on the other side.

SIX   THE WOUNDED WELKIN

I know more than Apollo,
For oft when he lies sleeping
I behold the stars at mortal wars
And the wounded welkin weeping;
The moon embrace her shepherd
And the queen of love her warrior,
While the first doth horn the star of morn
And the next the heavenly farrier
  Whiles that I sing, "Any food, any feeding,
  Money, drink or clothing?
  Come dame or maid, be not afraid—
  Poor Tom will injure nothing."
                              —Tom o' Bedlam's Song

XVI

AT FIRST THE incredible news which Saul Carpender broke to him stunned Dennis completely. He could not react to it—could only mechanically complete the motions he was going through, to dock his boat on the slipway Dan Sakky had carved from the rock. The drone of the engine peaked, to lift the craft on its hoverducts, then died as he shut off the power altogether. By that time, attracted by the noise, two others had joined Saul on the wharf, both looking weary, dirty, and dispirited.

And both, like Saul, carrying their guns.

The first was Yoko, her suit grimy in a way he had never expected to see. He had always known her to be fastidious about her appearance, smart as one of the ancient Japanese dolls she so much resembled. A bandage was wrapped around her left wrist.

A moment later Tibor Gyorgy emerged into view. The burly Magyar electronics expert was in the same state—hair tousled, beard growing out, his clothes unwashed for days, and armed. He was limping slightly, as though from a rheumaticky knee. Dull-faced, the three of them watched as Dennis got out of the boat and approached them.

"What in the world has been going on while I was away?" he demanded.

"Told you," Saul sighed. "Went off their heads, all six of them."

"Yes, but—"

So did I.

Dennis altered what he had been about to say. Time enough later to start on the mystery of how he had been able to stay alive, and return in good health, after ten days of apparently behaving like a mindless animal. He said, "But what did they actually *do?* Why are you in such a mess? Why are you carrying your guns all the time? How can six people out of a hundred and eighty make you look so—well, so downright *scared?*"

The three exchanged glances, as though embarrassed. At length Tibor said, "I guess it isn't them. Though I am scared, that's true. I'm worried half out of my skull. It's what this disgusting planet is doing to us. Look!"

He skinned up the leg of his suit to reveal the swollen state of his right knee. As the dawn light grew stronger, Dennis could see the tell-tale scurvy marks, and realised that it must be from the same cause that they all wore the same expression of hopeless frustration.

"You're all right," Yoko said. "Tai gave you a supply of vitamin pills to take while you were away."

"But I didn't use them up," Dennis said.

"Don't give us that!" Saul's voice was thick with contempt. "You can tell just by looking—*you* don't have any deficiency diseases!"

"I still have practically the whole jarful," Dennis insisted. "Here!" He turned to reach over the side of the boat and produced the jar as proof. "In any case, before I went away, Tai was saying he did have some of the ready-made stuff in store—he just didn't want to use it up before he absolutely had to, during the winter."

"Oh, sure, there's a bit of stock left. But not much. Not after Tai got to it and started throwing it away."

"*What?*"

"Fact. Here, give us some of them pills!" Saul extended his hand greedily.

"Well—well, sure!" Dennis uncapped the jar and handed it over. They each gulped one of the capsules and would have taken more, but that they looked accusingly at one another like shipwrecked sailors sharing out the last drops of fresh water on a raft.

Before he could speak again, someone else appeared from the direction of the village: a lean young coloured man with an aggressive expression, one of Ulla's junior mineralogists whose name he could not for a moment recall.

"Ah, Steve!" Yoko said with relief, and he remembered-Steven Highwood, that was it.

"The prodigal returned, him?" the Negro said, picking his way over the rocks. He too held his gun at the ready. "Well, I guess that's kind of good news. So we got one of the boats back."

"One of the boats back?" Dennis echoed, still confused.

"Sure. Why do you think we're mounting this guard rota?" Tibor sounded faintly surprised. "Or did you think we were spending the night out here by the harbour for fun, maybe? Kitty made off with one of the surviving cushionfoils, the one we'd stocked up to go and look for you in."

"That's right," Yoko chimed in. "I was due to go, and Steve, and Hal Bengtsson from Dan Sakky's section. And when I came down here with Saul first thing in the morning, to make a final check of it, she'd made off in it."

"Kitty did that?"

"Ah, hell! I never thought being out of touch for a few days would addle a bright guy's brains like this." Saul turned towards the village. "Let's go get some breakfast and we'll tell you the rest of it. There's too bloody much of it to get through right now. What's the grub like this morning, by the way, Steve?"

Settling on a convenient shelf of rock to survey the harbour, the young Negro shrugged. "Filthy slop, same as usual. But it plugs the gap. Go on—hurry. Or there may not be any left. The swine were practically eating the trough when I came away."

Breasting the rise and sighting the village closely for the first time since his return, Dennis stopped in his tracks. At one end of the barracks-like mess building, there was a jagged gap in the wall, and from it black smears, the traces of soot, licked up crazily.

He said, "What the—? Was there a fire?"

"What does it look like?" Tibor muttered. "Which of them did we have to thank for that, Saul? Dan, was it?"

"No, Ulla. It was Dan who smashed the dam and let the reservoir drain dry."

"What?" Dennis exclaimed.

"I keep telling you—they went crazy! Don't you understand?" Saul turned furious red-rimmed eyes on him.

"Saul, it must be a terrible shock for Dennis meeting all this at once," Yoko soothed. "We had it in separate stages, and that was bad enough. It happened this way, Dennis. About the second morning after you failed to call in, when we were all set to go looking for you, we got up to find that all the six test subjects were wandering around the village—delirious, I suppose. They were literally raving, talking about gods and devils, and goodness knows what. So we tried to calm them, of course, and eventually they seemed to become rational again, after several hours, except that they'd acquired an obsession. They kept trying to make everyone else go straight to the experimental plots and eat the fruit and vegetables. Which of course was a crazy idea. They were out of their minds. We caught one of them—I think it was Dan, wasn't it?" she interpolated with a glance at Tibor—"drinking unpurified water, and he tried to tell us that we must. Not *ought* to: *must*. In the end we decided we'd have to restrain them for their own good, but I suppose we tipped our hand. We thought we'd surprise them in their own rooms, which they went to normally at nightfall—apart from this insistence on making us eat native-grown food, they were behaving sanely in most respects—but before we caught them . . ."

She shrugged. "Well, I suppose it was our own fault for not warning *everybody*. Only the people who had spoken to them during the day realised they were crazy. We were afraid what might happen if the word got around. So, pretending to be in their right minds, they managed to commit acts of sabotage. Tai got into the biolab, smashed everything he could lay hands on, poured medicines and vitamins down the drain. Dan went out and wrecked all the purification filters on the water-pipes, and wound up by driving a tractor into the middle of the dam. It burst, and we don't expect to be able to fix it before the stormy season begins. Kitty made off with that boat, too, and we don't know what's become of her or it."

Dennis listened in icy misery, as though his heart had been replaced by a frozen stone.

"What about Parvati?" he demanded. "Did she—?"

"They all did. I don't know if they planned it together. But she wasn't the next one we caught. That was Ulla. She was mixing in native-grown food with the supplies that had been set out for breakfast. When they tried to stop her, she tipped one of the heaters over and started the fire you can still see the traces of. Then Abdul went to the *Niña* and shorted a high-tension powerlead through the girders so they lit up like the filament of one of those old light-bulbs—look!"

She threw up her arm, and Dennis saw that the shape of the *Niña* was deformed, its original smooth ovoid silhouette twisted as though the weight of a giant's foot had come down on it, crushingly.

"Blew out three of our generators!" Yoko said. "He'd shorted the current past the circuit-breakers. One of them exploded, and Tibor isn't certain he can repair the others."

Tibor uttered a sound which might have been a Magyar curse.

Dazed by the stream of disasters Yoko had been describing, Dennis fumbled for another question. Before he could put it, they had been spotted by people emerging from the mess-hall, who recognised him and came crowding around to demand what had happened to keep him away so long.

He said curtly, "I had a run-in with a sort of fish. I think it poisoned me. I must have been delirious for a bit." And, as they automatically shied away from him, suspicious of contagion, added: "But my medikit says I'm all right again now."

That provoked nods and shrugs, and almost as soon as they had assembled the people started to drift away again. It seemed that their apathy prevented them from being interested for very long. Dennis noted the marks of scurvy on them, and shuddered.

Does this mean we're going to have to evacuate? Can we evacuate? Or would everyone be so sick and undernourished before we reached Earth again that the attempt would be wasted?

"Well—ah—we've still got the *Santa Maria*, haven't we?" he said. "If the worst comes to the worst, we can always—"

"The worst has come to the worst," Yoko said gently. "I assume you were thinking of abandoning Asgard and trying to make it home? We can't, though. That's thanks to what Parvati did. She managed to get into the computer room and instructed the computers to blank their memories. All the navigational data, all the takeoff and landing data, all the life-support data

. . . Because of what she did to us, that big shining ship up there is just about as useful as a lump of dirt. It would take more than a lifetime to re-stock the memory banks with what they were filled with when they left Earth."

She wrung her hands and her small mouth turned downwards at the corners. After a moment, tears trickled from the corners of her slanted eyes.

"We're going to die here!" she forced out. "We're all going to die here! And I don't—want—to—die!"

XVII

STEVE HAD BEEN right: the food was slop. Sour-faced, their hands dirty, the dietitians ladled out portions of it so carelessly that some of it splashed on the counter from which the colonists lined up to collect it. It was some sort of warmed-through basic meal, or mush, salted. That was all. In answer to Dennis's expression of dismay, one of the servers said curtly, "Don't look at me like that! This is all we have left that's fit to eat!"

"It's not fit to eat," someone called from a nearby table.

"Safe, then! Safe!" the server snapped. "You know damned well what I mean!"

Behind the counter, with its big dishes steaming slightly, there was the smoke-grimed ruin of the food preparation plant. The wreckage had apparently been shoved to one side, and left. Had no one attempted to repair it, then?

It was not strictly the food the servers were throwing at him which dismayed Dennis. It was the underlying attitude implied by their willingness to make do with it. A horrid suspicion took root in the corner of his mind,

and grew. He sensed the irritability which he knew de-
rived, like the bruising and Tibor's swollen knee, from
the scurvy. The lethargy which the disease also entailed
was writ plain on every face he glanced at. With the
colony in a desperate plight, many people—thirty or
forty, perhaps—having long finished their breakfast,
were still dawdling over the tables: not talking, just sitting and sometimes staring at Dennis.

But they didn't even bother to come over and inquire
what had happened to him!

To have bitten this deep into the colonists' minds, the
leaching effect of their deficiency must already have set
in well before the last progress meeting. The cheering
news of their success must have masked inertia, a state
of coasting, in which people could keep going only so
long as they were following a rote pattern. Faced with
the urgent need to think for themselves, to diverge from
the standard plan and make shift, they were helpless.
All these people ought to have been out at work the
moment they had choked down the last spoonful of
their mush. Instead . . .

But he had only just walked into the middle of this
totally new situation. For the time being, Dennis decided he must move cautiously. The sudden baseless
anger which had flared in the server's face might
emerge in Saul's, or Tibor's.

At least these two, however, seemed to be willing to
talk sensibly.

"Hell, we're dirty and unshaven because that bastard
Dan smashed the water-filters and breached the reservoir!" Saul grunted. "We're getting just about enough
clean water to cook with and drink, from the remaining
purifiers. We don't have it over for washing clothes or
shaving."

But why shouldn't you wash in the water from the

stream? It's good natural spring water, what you get on Earth!

"We're going down hill fast," Tibor muttered. "That yellow devil Tai didn't content himself with messing up the biolab. Looks as though he set out deliberately to make us fall sick. Just pouring vitamins and medicines down the sink—that's what he must have been doing!"

Yet I went without for ten days, and here I am, in better shape than these two!

He glanced uneasily across the room towards Yoko, who had gone into a corner by herself after her outburst of misery, and remembered thinking that she had a life-time interest in her speciality, which would maintain her enthusiasm for study far past any risk of boredom.

Tibor said he was scared. So am I—so am I!

"But what have you been doing since all this—this sabotage took place?" he demanded. "Why is there still that heap of muck behind the counter in here? Why hasn't anyone patched the hole in the wall which the fire made?"

Saul and Tibor exchanged glances.

"Yes, I guess someone ought to have seen to that," Saul admitted after a pause.

"Someone!" Dennis thumped the table with his fist. The guns which the other two had laid down beside their plates jumped and rattled; his own was stowed in his pocket, as always. "Who's the someone if it's not going to be you?"

"Don't talk to me like that!" Tibor flared. "Haven't I got enough trouble of my own since that bastard Abdul shorted out all those generators? One of them blew up, like Yoko told you—the bits are scattered all over creation and most of them won't be any use again even if we find them."

"How much power does it take to fetch a stack of board from the sawmill and drive a couple of dozen nails?" Dennis rapped. And, struck by what Tibor had just said, he went on: "You don't mean you're actually spending your time hunting over the island for the bits of the generator that blew?"

"Well—why not?"

"Why not? You just told me why not! You said the parts won't be any good for re-use! Abdul didn't wreck the solar collectors, did he? There's still power going down the lines!"

"Won't be when the summer ends," Tibor said defensively.

"Hell, we knew that, didn't we? We knew that right along! What about the tidal generators you were supposed to be rigging?"

"We were going to build them out of scrap from the *Niña*, and—"

"And Abdul half-melted the whole shebang." Dennis drew a deep breath. "So why aren't you there building a—a water-wheel, for heaven's sake? They had electricity back on Earth a hundred years before they managed fission, let alone fusion. Didn't they?"

"Dennis, stop riding him," Saul said. "The kind of information you'd need for that went with the rest of the computer memories which Parvati blanked out. There's not much point in grousing about it. It's happened, and that's that."

"The hell it is! I'm not an expert on this kind of problem, but I've seen pictures. I could build a water-wheel without a computer telling me what to do!"

"Then get the hell out and build one, before I throw you out!" Tibor exploded, and leapt to his feet.

For an instant the scene froze. Even the apathetic faces surrounding them showed a spark of interest at the prospect of a fight. But Tibor's rage evaporated, and he subsided into his chair again, shaking his head.

"You only just got back here," he said in a whining

tone. "Can't expect you to understand what's really going on."

"That's true enough," Dennis grunted. "Far as I can see, just about six things have happened, and any of them could have arisen from natural causes instead of sabotage. Like water not coming out when you turn the faucet. Hell, we have buckets, don't we? People don't have to walk around stinking because they can't fetch a pail of water from the stream. And the dam was built once—why can't it be built again?"

"We haven't got Dan any longer," Saul said, exaggeratedly patient.

"But—!" Dennis said sharply. "The more you tell me, the sillier it all seems. When this happened, didn't you call a progress meeting and review the situation, allot new priorities, second repair teams from non-urgent jobs?"

Saul drew back defensively. "Well—ah—it was pretty obvious what was wrong, and there was no need to depress everybody by calling 'em together and talking about it."

"And what the hell kind of a progress meeting would it have been, anyway, when we'd been set back practically to square one?" Tibor put in.

Dennis shook his head dazedly. "This is ridiculous," he muttered. "Judging by this, we don't deserve to survive. What we'd have done in face of an earthquake, say—"

"Stuff that sort of talk!" Tibor ordered. "We're not going to survive anyhow, so what's the use?"

"The way you're letting things slide, you're right," Dennis agreed. "But I'm damned if I'm going to surrender without a fight! Who's chairing the colony now? Who's looking after admin?"

"Well, without Abdul and Parvati—" Saul began. Dennis cut him short, raising his hand.

"Thanks, that's all you had to say. And that's one thing that's going to change, for a start." He scooped up the last of his food, cold and tasteless, and thrust the plate away. "I'm going off to look over the island and see just how bad things really are. This kind of defeatism is nonsense!"

He rose and turned to go, scowling. Struck by a sudden thought, he hesitated.

"What have you done with them, by the way—the test subjects?"

"I ordered 'em locked up." Saul shrugged. "It was the best we could manage. Here, I'll take you along and show you." He too rose, and someone at an adjacent table stirred from apathy long enough to ask where he was going.

"To look at them," Saul said.

With the first approach to animation Dennis had seen since his return, the others in the mess-hall got to their feet with a clatter. They all moved out together in a disorderly stream and set off up the winding village street in the direction of the *Santa Maria*. Walking with the rest, Dennis noted still more terrifying things: one of Tai's aides crouched on a doorstep, asleep with his mouth open; a bucket of night-soil outside another door, unlidded, since presumably the lack of water to flush the drains . . .

But it's insane! It's literally and completely insane!

Also, as he was able to see when the street brought him higher, someone had been through a plot of Tai's experimental plants and chopped them off, leaving only the stems to rot in the sun. That couldn't have been sabotage. Yoko would have mentioned it. With the colony on the verge of starvation, what fool had spoiled potentially edible crops?

He was so preoccupied that it took a nudge from Tibor to bring him back to awareness. He realised that the group of people in whose midst he had come to this spot had fanned out, and with unaccountable enthusiasm were shouting and jeering in a blur of noise from which he could sort out only the inflections: mockery and rage.

What they were looking at was a cage, made of the steel reinforcement bars Dan used for building in concrete. In the cage, on its bare floor, were sitting the test subjects.

They were all quite naked, and for lack of any facilities the floor was patched with their filth, but they were erect and alert, although thin with privation. Compared to those who mocked from beyond the bars, they were paragons of human dignity.

"Ain't been any change since we put them in there," Saul was saying. "We hoped the effects would wear off—whatever they were—but I came up here only yesterday to try and get Tai to tell us what we ought to do to fix these swollen joints everyone's getting now, and he was going on same as before about eating those damned poisonous plants of his, so I sent someone to chop 'em down, and . . ."

The voice went on. Dennis stopped listening. He was staring at the figures within the cage: Dan Sakky nearest him, like an ebony Buddha; in the centre Abdul, upright as an ancient Pharaoh; next Parvati, graceful and delicate as an antelope, the look of resignation on her face slipping momentarily as she spotted and recognized him. She made a gesture to indicate the people gathered around, raised her hand to her temple and described a circle there, and unexpectedly winked at him, as to say: *What do these silly little folk think they're playing at?*

A sudden blast of white-hot fury engulfed Dennis. He strode forward, clawing at the pocket of his suit which held the gun he had never before removed except for testing. "Hey!" someone exclaimed. "What the—?"

"Get out of the way or you'll fry, and I shan't weep," Dennis said between his pale, stiff lips. He set the muzzle of the gun for a flat fan-shaped beam.

"Dennis!" Saul said, hurrying after him. "What are you going to do?"

"You ordered these people caged?"

"Well—what else could we do? We—"

"You could have tried a little pity, a little decency, just as a start."

"After what they did to us? Hell, we couldn't risk them breaking loose, doing more damage, busting up more of what we've built!" Saul was almost gibbering.

Dennis levelled the gun. On every side, people drew back, shivering and whispering. When they were clear of his line of fire, he set the gun parallel to the nearest side of the cage. The occupants rose to their feet and stepped as far out of range as they could.

He pressed the trigger, and metal ran down like quicksilver. The bars, under tension, snapped in succession, each with a baritone singing noise. A second cut, and there was a gap wide enough to climb through. Dennis turned the gun-muzzle towards the watchers. Behind him, one by one, the prisoners scrambled into freedom. The last to leave was Parvati. He felt the soft touch of her hand on his nape, but dared not turn his head from surveying the group who had locked the unfortunates up.

"Thank you," she breathed. "You too must have seen the truth—I don't know how. We failed to show it to them. You try. We'll be around to help as much as we can."

And she loped off after her companions, who had already taken the straightest possible line out of the village and towards the wild country on the higher slopes of the island's central hill.

"Right!" Dennis said, when he was sure they had

had a chance to make their escape. "Saul, go to the admin office and sound the siren for a general meeting. I don't know how much longer you planned to carry on down this roller-coaster slide to disaster, but I'm quitting right here and I'm going to take the ones who have the guts with me. The rest, for all I or the planet Asgard care, can rot in their skins. *Move!*"

XVIII

SULLENLY, YET WITH a curious air of relief, as though they had been silently hoping for someone to take them in charge, the colonists assembled for the meeting. At first the early arrivals just stood about on the surface of the street. On all previous occasions, they had voluntarily gone into the mess-hall and fetched seating. This time, it took the lash of Dennis's scorn to stir them to the effort.

"Well? Want to stand up for the whole of this session? It's going to be a long one, but it's up to you!"

Shamefaced, they moved to fetch the chairs and benches. With much irritable cursing they eventually got them into the normal arrangement. Meantime, as though wishing to propitiate this energetic demon who had materialised in their midst, Saul and Tibor had brought the chairman's table from the admin office, and set three chairs behind it facing the crowd. Apparently, without coming into the open and staking a direct claim, Saul had been nursing secret ambitions to exercise authority—witness his claim to have ordered the imprisonment of the test subjects. But he merely hovered around, at the back of the table, as though afraid that if he took the middle chair, the seat of honor, Dennis would order him out of it.

For his part, Dennis ignored him. He had liked Saul at least as well as all the other people whom chance had landed him among. To discover that he was capable of such an inhuman act as creating a kind of public Bedlam for a group of unfortunates temporarily out of their minds, so that his companions could come and mock them, had filled him with a sick distrust of any human being.

And I'm not even sure I can trust myself, after the ten lost days . . .

But fresh in his memory was the puzzling whisper he had heard from Parvati as she climbed out of the cage. What did she mean by "the truth"? Yet she had seemed hopeful of his ability to save the colony, and promised help, and whatever insanity had gripped the test subjects it had obviously passed.

Any earnest of support, in a plight like this, was welcome. He decided to accept it for what it was worth, and plough his own furrow.

The colonists took their places, hardly talking to one another: all without exception dirty, many ragged as well, having snagged their clothes and not bothered to attempt repairs. Scurvy had branded their skins. Yet somewhere in the distant past men so weak with scurvy they could hardly stand had fought four-masted windjammers around Cape Horn in the teeth of a winter gale, and those were ignorant gutter-sweepings, not the cream of Earth's best-trained minds. It might no longer be possible to maintain the Asgard colony, but if they had to go home, at least they needn't go home like cringing puppies!

He did a fast count by eye. Ten minutes after the siren, and a good thirty people not yet present. He noticed Saul glancing at him, and turned his head inquiringly.

"Shall I call them to order?" Saul proposed.

"The hell! Where are the others?"

"You want to wait for them? Shall I sound the siren again?"

"No!" Dennis drew a deep breath. He scanned the audience in search of someone who seemed less overwhelmed by apathy than the average, and his gaze fell on Steven Highwood. "You, Steve! Know where to find some paint?"

"Well—yes, I guess so."

"Right. We're going to do something they did in ancient Greece. Get that paint and a rope's end. Go and find every lazy son of a bitch you can't shift off his ass to come and talk about the rescue of this community, and whip paint all over his stinking body. And nobody with paint comes into mess-hall until it's worn off him. That clear? If I have to I'll stand at the door myself and keep them out. Move!"

Steve cocked a surprised eyebrow. "Sounds like a system, man," he acknowledged, and headed down the street.

Five minutes passed. There was a commotion, and they looked around to see the missing colonists coming at a stumbling run, followed by the grinning Steve flailing his paint-smeared rope. As they fell into their seats, he called out, "That's the lot except for Silvana Borelli—she's laid up with a bad ankle and can't walk. I said I'd go tell her what happened afterwards. That okay?"

"That's okay," Dennis confirmed, and strode over to the table. For a long moment he hesitated. Then he picked up two of the three chairs, one in each hand, and held them out at arm's length to Saul and Tibor.

I may be making deadly enemies, but we can't let this go on!

"Here—take these and get out there with everyone else!" he ordered. "You seem to have been more or less running things lately, and what's happened as a result is a downright disgrace."

Stunned, the two men simply stared at him, making no move to take the chairs.

"Don't you agree?" Dennis threw at the audience. "Look at yourselves! You're filthy! You stink! You've behaved more like primitives out of the Dark Ages than civilised people—going and jeering at lunatics for a Sunday outing!"

"Right!" Steve Highwood shouted, and after a fearful pause there was a mutter of embarrassed agreement. White as paper, without taking the chairs, Saul and Tibor moved to places on the general benches.

"Okay, we'll keep these chairs here as a sort of Siege Perilous," Dennis declared, letting them drop to the ground again. "It's open to anyone to come and take them over, but on one condition—they prove themselves capable of coping with the responsibility it involves. That's the same condition I'm here on! Let's get that straight right away, shall we? For example"—he drew up the chairman's chair to the table and went on talking in a more conversational tone—"I just said you were filthy. You are. Why?"

"Well, when Dan broke the dam—" Tibor began defensively.

"Stuff that immediately," Dennis cut in, taking malicious pleasure in throwing Tibor's own phrase back at him. "How many dams did Dan build on other islands? I've been away from piped and purified water for almost four weeks. I didn't even have buckets and tanks—I used the cushionfoil's inflatable dinghy for a bath-tub! First thing after this meeting, the whole gang of us is going to the stream with soap and disinfectant. Steve, keep that painted rope handy—and watch out particularly for the mess-hall staff! I never expected to see anyone handling food with black-edged fingernails in *my* lifetime!"

Several people shifted as though trying to sit on their hands and hide them. Dennis concealed a grin.

"Right! Now one more thing we've got to straighten out before we can get to real work. We're short of power, but we aren't without it—we're short of scrap but we aren't without it—we're short of water but we aren't without it—and so on and so on. Any or all of these things could have happened through a natural disaster. True or false? This is a tectonically active world; we seem to have hit it during a quiescent stage, but the process isn't over. We could have had an earthquake which tipped the *Santa Maria* off that peak it's sitting on and sent it rolling through the village like a ball down a bowling-alley. Did you ever think of that? I did! I came here before, remember, and there were exactly four of us, and if what happened to the *Pinta* had happened to the *Argo* there wouldn't have been anyone left to pick up the pieces and make the sacrifice worth while. You're a standing bloody mockery of what those people up there on the moon gave their lives for—aren't you?"

Dead silence followed.

Suddenly Yoko leapt to her feet, clenching her small fists. "What's the good?" she forced out. "What's the *good?* We shan't be able to live here—the best we can hope for is to die!"

"And weren't your ancestors Samurai?" Dennis said cuttingly. "Or were they mud-grubbing peasants, and nothing more?"

The insult went through Yoko's hysteria like a bullet through butter. She took possession of herself again like an invading army, letting her hands fall quietly to her sides.

"Yes," she muttered. "Yes, I should have under-stood." And she resumed her seat.

"Just in case that particular truth hasn't penetrated yet," Dennis said after a pause, "and just in case there's anyone still pinning his hopes on returning to Earth in the *Santa Maria*, I guess I should point out that I'm the only person here who's ever tried flying a qua-space ship manually. In fact I held the record when we left Earth—it's not something I often boast about, but it's a fact, for what it's worth. And you know what that record was?"

He waited.

"Earth-orbit to Mars-orbit with an error of less than eight per cent. At that point we quit. You *can't* fly a qua-space ship on human reflexes. The instruments don't exist which can convert qua-space information into forms we can handle. You need the nanosecond reflexes of automatics. And we don't have the automatics any longer. Their data-banks have been cleaned out. In any case, though, since we didn't have enough ascorbic acid to carry us through a winter here, we don't have enough to keep us going through a trip back to Earth. We're not Earthfolk any longer. We're citizens of Asgard. And isn't that what you wanted? Or were you fooling me?"

Once more he waited, wondering whether it was only the apathy which stemmed from scurvy that was re-straining the audience from telling him to go to hell, or whether he was genuinely reaching their self-respect.

"I take it you agree with me," he said finally. "So the next step is to find out just how badly off we are, instead of wringing our hands and moaning. Who's taken over biological section in Tai Men's place?"

There was a stir among the biologists, but no reply.

"Nobody there with enough guts to take charge and make plans?" Dennis clapped his hand to his forehead.

"Then find someone, and do it fast! And the same goes for all the other sections who've lost their chiefs. By this time tomorrow I want a complete breakdown of our supplies, our most urgent tasks, our necessary repair jobs, our known natural resources and our secondary skills. Even if it's only darning clothes, I want to know who can do what and teach others to do it!"

"Sure!" Saul said grumpily. "And we fix things, and what happens? Those damned lunatics you turned loose will come along and sabotage them all over again!"

Dennis looked him straight in the eye. "The way I heard it all my life," he said, "delusions of persecution are the symptom of a worse kind of insanity than any those poor devils you locked up were suffering from. There are six of them and a hundred and seventy-five of us. If they're on the winning side, then—hell's name—I'm inclined to go join them! All right, meeting adjourned to the same time tomorrow. And let's hear some sense talked then, shall we?"

SEVEN WHAT THE PANTHER DARE NOT

The Gypsy Snap and Pedro
Are none of Tom's comrados.
The punk I scorn and the cutpurse sworn
And the roaring boys' bravadoes.
The sober, white, and gentle,
Me trace or touch, and spare not,
But those that cross Tom's rhinoceros
Do what the panther dare not
*   Although I sing, "Any food, any feeding,*
*   Money, drink or clothing?*
*   Come dame or maid, be not afraid—*
*   Poor Tom will injure nothing."*
*   —Tom o' Bedlam's Song*

XIX

"NOW WE'LL HAVE this out of the way for a start! The fire can't have done it much harm—take it outside and sort it. Get a bucket of water to wash the grime off."

"But all that grease—"

"We have soap left, don't we? Or get a shovelful of beach sand! Do I have to tell you everything?"

"This is going to make a hell of a draught come winter! Cover it over. Doesn't matter how it looks—just cover it."

"But—"

"There are planks in stock at the sawmill, aren't there?"

"But nails!"

"Hell, the planks which are burned through were fixed by nails in the first place, weren't they? Ease 'em out and use 'em again!"

"But they'll be bent!"

"Oh, for—! Look, *moron,* you get a flat piece of stone and bang the nails on it until they're straight again. Do I have to show you everything?"

"It's not going to be arctic here during the winter, but it's going to be chilly come the turn of the year. These rooms of ours are badly insulated. Start gathering the branches of these shrubs. Take one of the cushion-foils and bring a cargo or two of them back from other islands. Lay 'em out to dry in the sun and wind."

"But I don't see—"

"Look, you fasten them together in a sort of mat, see? Then you lash it to the inside of the wall and all

141

over the ceiling, and it traps the warm air like clothes. You get it now, or do I have to construct a working model?"

"Wire rope? What for? Oh—yes, I remember Kitty warning us about the fall gales. And Dan did say we'd need guys. And we don't have any, hm? Let's think about that for a bit, then . . . Got it! Weights. They'll do for the time being. Plenty of good heavy rocks down by the sea. Lay 'em along the line of the walls so their weight is transmitted straight down and doesn't bow the roof. We made those beams pretty thick, fortunately."

"Yes, I *know* we were supposed to adapt the bearings from that gadget and it's been distorted out of round! So what? Can't you rig a treadle-operated lathe and true them back? At least well enough for them to turn in a bed of grease?"

"But you can't grind hard steel on a wooden treadle lathe! What do you use for a tool?"

"Lord! Go cannibalise one of the rock-drill bits! A diamond ought to be hard enough, surely?"

"Now we can expect the peak winter tides to fill that little natural basin. If we take the drain from it past a water-wheel—"

"But there isn't a channel for it to follow!"

"So *make* one! Look, run it over that lip there—see? Then rig a bucket-wheel under the rim, so the flow turns it continually."

"But that won't deliver the voltage we—"

"Hell's name, of *course* it won't! This is for our back-up power stocks. It's not designed to feed the whole village, only to charge accumulators. Then with the power from the accumulators, if we don't drain them for emergencies in any given day, we split water—

electrolyse it—and refill the hydroxy fuel cells on things like the tractors and the cushionfoils, so they'll always be available for use. And we certainly are not going to freeze in our rooms, either! Or eat cold food in the middle of winter! Blazes, we have the cream of Earthside technical skills to make the best of the materials we have to hand!"

"Does it burn?"

"What?"

"I said does it burn? Combust? Oxidise under controllable conditions? You want to eat nothing but cold food all winter? Nor do I. So does it burn and give off a hot flame? The kitchen equipment won't go back to power-operation until we find a suitable insulator for the cables, which all got scorched off in the fire. But that equipment was designed so it could be converted to burn wood if the need arose."

"How did you know? Information like that—"

"No, I didn't sift through the data-banks in the computers before Parvati wiped them! I just looked at the equipment, that's all. The heater bars can double as a grate, with gaps for the ash to fall through into a pan underneath; rip out the useless metal bits of the cable, and you've got flame-channels running up the sides of the vats. All that remains is to couple them to a chimney. You know what a chimney is, or must I draw you a picture?"

More exhausted than he had ever dreamed of being in his life, yet somehow managing to keep going when his eyes were sunk deep into pits in his face, rimmed with red but alight with the fire of single-minded dedication, Dennis hurled answers to questions at everyone who came begging. Some of them were wrong—the ash from burning native plants didn't react with grease in the proper way to make soap, for example, so he had to send people off in search of substitutes, like pumice, or fuller's earth—but most were right, and as the days leaked away he grew more and more astonished at what he was managing to dredge up from his subconscious.

All the sections which had lost their leaders had done as he said, and found replacements: Steve Highwood had moved into Ulla Berzelius's slot right away; a portly, cheerful woman called Ellen Shikalezi from Botswana had managed to get the biomedical section operating again; the meteorological section was working on a routine basis anyhow, and Kitty's former senior aide, Hugh Lauriston, was willing enough to handle the storm-warning side—the only really crucial part—on his own, turning loose his two colleagues for other duties; while the girl who had been Dan Sakky's architectural programmer, Zante Ionescu, quietly set about designing the makeshifts Dennis called for and found herself *de facto* in charge of construction after a week or so.

He himself, of course, had combined Abdul's and Parvati's jobs by accident, and there was no one to take over from him.

But what plagued him far worse than simple tiredness was the curious situation which recurred and recurred all the time he was shaking people and kicking them into activity.

Although, thanks to the training which had gone into the months prior to his original visit, with the four-man *Argo* team, he probably had a wider range of available survival data than any other single person on Asgard, he had never expected to be able to tell specialists things about their own disciplines which they knew themselves and had never thought of in the present context. Typically, he listened to an allegedly insoluble problem, thought for a few moments, and said, "What about . . . ?"

Whereupon the specialist hit his or her forehead with open palm and said, "Why didn't I think of that?"

Why indeed? Granted, there was scurvy rampant among the colonists, so their minds must inevitably be dulled, but after much heart-searching he had reached a compromise with Ellen: anyone whose joints began to swell should receive a ration of ascorbic acid to keep them going. By now, every colonist had been allotted at least one rescue dose, and many were on what amounted to supportive therapy, requiring massive doses every other day if they were to function at all.

Yet it wasn't merely that the minds of these brilliant specialists were sluggish. Dennis reached that conclusion after he had been able to show a dozen or more of them how to exploit their own knowledge to best advantage.

It's more as though I look at Asgard from a different standpoint.

He wished achingly that Parvati were available to discuss this question with him. He was beginning to formulate an explanation, but he lacked the background to judge something as fundamental as a cultural shift. He could only hypothesise that whereas in the ultimate analysis the colonists had a vague vision of building a replica of the Earth they had left behind, for which they could take unique credit, he with his explorer's mentality looked on the predicament he was in more as a matter of survival, regardless of the purpose for which he was to survive. He seemed to be looking at the potential of Asgard, a whole new planet; they, at the ways in which Asgard fell short of the Earthly ideal.

But consideration of abstract matters like that would have to wait. There were plenty of more concrete problems to which he had even less of a solution.

For instance: there was one exception to the rule that the colonists were weak and lethargic, needing to be jarred into action, and kept going on heavy additional doses of ascorbic acid. That exception was himself.

Lying alone at night in his room, he pondered that mystery endlessly. Ever and again he was driven to the inescapable conclusion that the key to it must lie in the ten lost days by himself on that other distant island. Logic said that he had blindly eaten, or perhaps drunk, some naturally occurring substance which compensated for the effect of the debilitating bacterium that infected them all. He was eating the same diet as everyone else here, yet he alone had been able to decline the offer of synthetic vitamin supplements.

He tried to reassure himself with the recollection of his positive achievements. People acknowledged them, and sometimes shyly said they were grateful. The food was being properly cooked again, and one of the dietitians had discovered her talent as a chef, so that it was actually appetising. People were clean, and while he hadn't yet been able to spare the time or manpower to rebuild the reservoir and supply running water again, he had been able to organise a delivery system by mounting a metal tank from the *Niña* on the back of a tractor, and the laundry could be done and the toilets could be flushed with disinfectant, albeit by hand.

Yet he was pursued into his dreams by guilty knowledge which often brought him awake sweating and trembling. He, and no one else in the village, had somehow found out how to escape the plague of scurvy. And unless he was able to share this secret with the others, he was going to watch them did, helplessly. He was going to be an Adam without an Eve.

Unless . . .

XX

FOR A WHILE, his sheer energy was enough to maintain his authority over the others. Even Saul, who had been publicly insulted far worse than Tibor—because everyone conceded that elaborations like electronics must take second place to essentials like food and shelter—grudgingly decided to cooperate, and forwent his speciality to lend a hand where he was needed, in the same way as Dennis had done following their arrival.

But he began to sense a growing disquiet when his preoccupation with the mystery of his own good health led him to inquire what had become of the test subjects.

Briefly, when he recovered his senses on the diamond island—as he now thought of it—he had been angered by the realisation that no one had come to search for him. Now, trapped in an endless maze of immediate problems, he was compelled to admit that he was capable of the same neglect. He had seen and heard nothing of them since he set them free from their cage. He had promised himself that he would make arrangements for their welfare; they must be found, fed, if humanly possible helped to return to their place in the community.

Then everything fell on him, as though the moon had been pitched from the sky, and there was never the time to decide how to tackle the job, nor the spare person who could be assigned to carry it out.

That reminds me: I used to be haunted by the moon, where my hope of return to Earth was smashed to bits. I haven't given it a thought for days. I don't even know what phase it's reached right now!

Perhaps that was a symbol of the way the change he

had deliberately set out to force in the minds of the
other colonists—by now he no longer separated himself
from them—was working in his own brain. He was
trying to get rid of every association with the security of
Earth, the ultimate refuge and escape route. It seemed
logical to encourage the subconscious acceptance of the
truth he had tried to drive home at the first progress
meeting he called: that they were not now Earthfolk,
but citizens of Asgard. He had abolished the nightly
watch in the *Santa Maria,* though prudence had prevented him from suggesting that it be cannibalised in
place of the *Niña,* much of which was now mere scrap-
heap thanks to Abdul. Also he had made the meetings
weekly instead of monthly. Asgard's moon followed a
thirty-six day cycle, not the twenty-nine day cycle of an
Earthly month; the month as a unit of time was therefore
irrelevant. It was, in a word, *alien.*

However, that had not been in the forefront of his
thoughts when he instituted the change. He felt rather
that the colonists needed encouragement. To be rein-
forced in their decisions by news of successes from
other sections: that was part of the fundamental attitude on which the colony's administration had always
been predicated. Yet as the time seeped away it became
more and more plain to him that this meed of encouragement was like the supportive doses of ascorbic acid
they were taking. It was a crutch, at best, enabling the
crippled community to take another half-step forward,
but next time it would be a half of a half-step, and
then . . .

*Zeno, damn you! Come here and reassure us that
Achilles did beat the tortoise in the end!*

And, finally, the day arrived which he had known in
his heart of hearts must come—the day when Ellen Shikalezi entered the admin office, now his headquarters,

without preamble, and told him that the supply of ascorbic acid had run out.

He pushed back his chair and looked for a long time through the unglazed window of the office. Window-glass was one of the things they had classified as luxuries; when the worst cold of winter hit them, they would make do by boarding the windows over. There would be power for one fluorescent lamp per room, at least.

If we live into the winter . . .

Beyond the hole in the wall, clouds scudded across the sky. Over to the east, some of them had shredded into an amorphous mass. There was going to be their first rainstorm some time within the next sixty hours, according to the forecasts.

I've almost forgotten what rain on a roof sounds like!

And there too was a clue to what must be done, but like all the others it eluded him. Sighing, he turned his attention back to Ellen. She was a plump, very dark woman, with what must ordinarily have been a motherly air, but now it was rather grandmotherly. She had lost a tooth owing to the scurvy weakening her gums, and she had settled herself stiffly in her chair thanks to the pain of her swollen joints.

"I guess we've been over all the alternatives," he said at length.

"There's one alternative," Ellen said. "That we use the native-grown crops. Since you tore that monumental strip off Saul for ordering some of the crops chopped down, we've kept them going—but more as a kind of ritual than for any practical purpose."

Ritual? The word seemed pregnant with unspoken meaning. Once more he failed to identify the concept he was groping after, and resumed talking.

"They'd provide what we need?"

"Tai said they would." Ellen shrugged. "Me, I've been sort of busy. I didn't re-check his findings. Couldn't, after the mess he made of the biolab."

Dennis hesitated. Suddenly he said, "You know something curious? I never thought of it before. But I guess you could have predicted who was most likely to take over as a replacement section chief, like yourself. It's turned out to be the people who didn't instantly forget everything they ever learned from the six we lost, just because they went out of their heads owing to—well, whatever it was."

"But you don't push it too hard," Ellen said wisely. "I noticed the same thing. Most of us have this big mental block developing, don't we? Saul's a prime example, but you get it from everyone to some degree."

"How do you mean—you don't push it?"

Ellen shrugged. "I was thinking of what happened at the meeting when you tried to get people to take an interest. That didn't work out so well, did it?"

"Damned right it didn't," Dennis admitted and thought back to that climactic moment when he had come close to losing his hard-won grip on the colonists' minds.

Was it the second meeting, or the third, after his return? Or was it—? Never mind! He had been plagued, as usual, during the previous night, by the thought that simply turning loose the captives from Saul's cage-Bedlam was not a service to them. By now they might have starved, drowned, died in any of fifty ways. And casting them out of the community altogether smacked too much of using them as scapegoats for his liking.

It wasn't fair—that was the basis of his attitude. All right, accept the likeliest assumption: that something in the native-grown vegetables and fruits they had sampled had driven them insane—even that their derangement was becoming permanent, as Saul believed—did that instantly afflict them with some sort of magical taboo, rendering them untouchable? They were still human, for pity's sake!

Saul maintained that, because when he tried to consult Tai about the deficiency they were suffering from the biologist insisted on the same solution as he had offered before, the five of them and hence presumably Kitty as well were hopelessly out of their senses.

Yet I myself . . .

That was something he had not dared mention to anyone, even Ellen. He could have spoken of it to Parvati; he could have come clean to her, and instead of hiding behind a fuzz of prevarications about his successful hunt for diamonds and a passing illness due to toxaemia, could have told her that he went mad for ten mortal days.

But his grip on the irritable, weak, depressed colonists was too precarious for him to be honest about that. Someone might have said, next time he lost his temper, that they were in the charge of a crazy man and might just as well have stuck with Abdul. Indeed, when he raised the question of the test subjects at the meeting, that was very nearly what Saul did say. He heard the voices in memory, shrill with anger.

"Who cares what's become of them?"

"But—"

"Let 'em rot! They ruined months of hard work that we sweated and slaved over! Are we to invite them back, say, 'Pretty please, come and smash some more of the things we need to stay alive'? Good riddance, that's what I think!"

"That's right! That's right!"

"Yes, but they were testing something which could have meant life or death to—"

"So what? Death's better than going out of your mind, isn't it? And where do we find the spare re-

sources to cope with crazy people who can't work to
support themselves?"

Luckily, from that embryonic red herring, he had
been able to steer the argument to a review of resources. But he knew it had been a close call. He had
not again dared to raise the question in a general meeting, though he had discreetly inquired of everyone he
encountered as he made his regular surveys of the island whether they had seen any sign of the missing six.

Nobody had—or at any rate, nobody admitted to it.
By now, therefore, it was reasonable to assume that Asgard had claimed its own first human lives, as though
jealous of its smaller rival the moon, which had claimed
so many and so soon.

And in a little while . . .

He shied away from the premonitive vision of
corpses on the thresholds of their homes, of the gradual
rotting of the roofs and walls they had laboured to
erect, of the ultimate ground-shiver in response to
mountain-building elsewhere on the planet which would
indeed shake the *Santa Maria* loose and scatter the rel-
ics of man like skittles. Then a tsunami would come,
and wash the fragments into the depths of the sea, and
there, in some unimaginable future, an as-yet unevolved
Asgard scientist would puzzle over scraps of incorrodible
metal and be laughed at by his respectable colleagues
for hypothesising a visitation from outer space . . .

"I've got to go off by myself and think," he said
harshly, and thrust his chair back. Heedless of her at-
tempts to stop him, he strode out of the room and
walked blindly up the flank of the nearest ridge.

From then on, for hours, he wandered about the island, avoiding more than the curtest of exchanges with
the people he met. The noon siren sounded for mess,

and he ignored it, welcoming the additional isolation it brought him because everyone else converged on the village.

Maybe we could save the time it takes to walk to and from work if we packaged the food and delivered it on site . . . ? What's the point, though? We're all going to die! We're not going to leave anything behind except bones!

Weary to the marrow, he sat down on a woodplant overlooking almost all the traces of man's temporary presence on Asgard. Was all this to be for nothing— was it all to be destroyed by the chance action of wind and weather?

His mind, like the day, darkened with clouds of murky grey. Distracted, he picked with his fingers at the soft, almost spongy bark of the woodplant he was sitting on, tearing free fragments and toying with them. That a venture on which people had expended their best efforts and their most precious hopes should be doomed because of a tiny bacterium—

His thoughts broke off in mid-flow. He drew his hand away from his mouth, to which it had strayed, and stared in dismay at what he saw. The bit of bark which he had been chewing was dark with his saliva, and there were little woody shreds of it between his teeth, which his tongue sought to dislodge.

Am I crazy, doing a thing like that?

Horrified, he was about to hurl the thing from him, when a voice spoke from nowhere, tinged with a chuckle of approval.

"I thought so! I don't know how you found out, but it was clear that you'd learned the truth."

He snapped his head around to the right, and saw Parvati, half-hidden among the jumbled boulders that spined the ridge: eyes sparkling, face glowing with

health, mouth turned upward in a smile. Jumping to his
feet in amazement, he called to her, but all she did by
way of reply was to blow him a kiss. Then she dodged
away among the rocks, and by the time he reached the
spot where he had seen her, she had disappeared.

XXI

FOR AN INFINITE age he stood staring stupidly from the
bare ground, where he was sure he had seen her, to the
fragment of bark in his hand, and back again. Had she
really been here, or had his overloaded mind generated
a delusion?

Or . . . ?

The third possibility was so paradoxical it braked his
thinking to a dead halt, as though he were plodding
through quicksand and had grown totally exhausted.
Logic insisted on telling him the concept was nonsensi-
cal, yet instinct declared that this was the only correct
alternative of the three.

Both.

Baffled, he felt a lunatically disproportionate sense
of frustration, as when everything else must stop because of a need to sneeze, yet the sneeze will not come.
He tried to explain to himself how it might be possible
for an event to be simultaneously real and unreal, because something below consciousness was telling him
that this was tremendously important, but he came no
closer to it than a hornet-swarm of apparently random
associations: from his ancestral heritage, the *síd;* from
his technical training, the weird mechanics of qua-
space; from his elementary education, the arguments of
relativity; from the recent past, a promise in Parvati's
voice about there being more traps on Asgard than any-

one had yet fallen into . . .

His hand was still reflexively clutching the scrap of bark he had been absently chewing. What could possibly account for such a stupid act as . . . ?

Click!

Once, a very long time ago, on a beach not far from where he was now standing, there had been a tall, rather graceful if not especially beautiful, and extremely sensible young woman named Sigrid Kallela, and a man a few years older, tough, equally sensible, named Dennis Malone. And something had come storming out of his subconscious like a hound of hell, chasing him away from all rationality and into a state of basic animality.

Why were there high fences and strong cages to contain the experimental animals they kept here?

Why were there only terrestrial test animals, when for a century the men of Earth had farmed and herded the creatures of the sea?

Why, when there was nothing on the whole of Asgard as far as had been determined more advanced than a squid or a codfish—nothing at all to compare with a dolphin or an elephant—was there precisely one group among the colonists dignified with the status of an independent section under its own section chief and yet not directly concerned with the establishment of survival of the colony: that one being the xenobiological section?

Why are we afraid of animals?

Very deliberately, he raised the scrap of bark to his mouth again and started to chew, considering the flavour. It was no way strange, despite the fact that he could call to mind no earthly comparison. It was pungent like nutmeg, but it was not nutmeg; it was bitter, like oil of almonds, but it was not oil of almonds; it was fragrant, like orange-peel, but it was not orange-peel . . .

Never mind. It was familiar. It assuaged a hunger far too deep for words.

Gradually, as he masticated the woody bark and swallowed the juice from it, his thinking clarified. Instead of the wild grab-bag of associations which had welled up a few minutes before, he found himself drawing perfectly sensible analogies to his experience, from soberly learned historical facts. He spat out a few stringy remnants and looked around for a fresh piece, not realising until after he had selected one that he had had some standard of judgment by which to make his choice: bark of a particular colour and sheen, something told him, was better than the rest.

Was this why he had been able to go on reasoning, improvising, making shift, when everyone else was lost in a fog of impotence? Could be—why not? After all, there were precedents, and he could now call them to mind with as much precision as an instructor briefing a class.

For example, during the preparation for the *Argo* flight, he and his companions had been crammed with information about survival problems. The data came from every period of history and every kind of civilisation, and in some cases from beyond civilisation. He had been told about the Australian aborigines and their use of *pithuri;* he had been told about the Bedouin tricks of steeping liquorice stalks in their drinking-water because it cut down water-loss by restricting urination; he had been told about the first lunar settlers, and long-voyage explorations which carried men to Pluto, and many, many more.

Somewhere in with the rest he had been told about one of the pioneer round-the-world trips by a nuclear submarine, following which the crew came ashore with an inexplicable need to eat cottage cheese. A check showed that they were short of calcium, and their bodies knew what they consciously did not: that this was the quickest way to replenish their supply.

Meditatively chewing on the bark of an alien plant, Dennis contemplated the ways in which the animal was wiser than the man.

At length he started to walk towards the shore. He chose his direction in the same reflexive fashion as he had chosen the right piece of bark to put in his mouth. That way lay the nearest of the other uncountable islands on the face of Asgard. He passed a few of his companions, tiredly going through the motions of tending the crops which they had brought here to plant, yet refused to eat, and accorded them no more than a curt nod. They for their part were too debilitated to spend time wondering why.

Eventually he came to the sea, peeling off his suit as he went, and threw it aside as he crossed the tide-line. He strode out into the shallows. Someone behind him seemed to have noticed what he was doing, because he heard a voice raised, shrill with complaint, which said something about trying to stop him. But although the cry was succeeded by the noise of running feet, before the pursuit reached the water's edge he was a hundred yards out and swimming strongly, and when he glanced back he saw a group of five or six men and women clustered there on the beach, not daring to come after him.

And yet, sooner or later, they must, or the fiction of man's conquest of Asgard would remain—a fiction.

Keeping a wary eye out for the species of water-creature with red fronds dangling beneath it which had stung him when he went swimming from the diamond island, although he doubted whether a second dose of the poison would have the spectacular consequences of the first one, he forged steadily through the clear water towards his goal. He met several of the native species, but most sheered away from him, as though whatever element of alienness their organs enabled them to sense from him alarmed them. A pretty greenish beast with a sort of sail, vaguely akin to a Portuguese man-o'-war, was too busy shedding its autumnal crop of egg-purses to worry about tacking out of his way, so he paid it the courtesy of making a short detour. The sun was still well above the horizon, however, when he reached the beach of the island he was aiming for and was able to stand up.

Now let's see . . .

This time, naturally, he was not relying on instinct; land was the normal habitat of human beings, and they operated by other, additional factors. It came quite automatically, though, to slip from the instinctual mode into the rational one, and ten minutes' walk through low scrub-like country brought him to a sheltered spot on the lee of a ridge similar to those on the base island.

There he encountered Dan Sakky, quite naked, squatting on his hunkers and probing with curious fingers into a hole-riddled area on the flank of a woodplant, where parasites had bored deep and starved the xylem of sap. Occasionally he withdrew one of the creatures, sniffed it, and tossed it aside.

"Dan!" Dennis said explosively, and strode forward. At the sound, the big dark man jerked his head around suspiciously, and he found himself looking into a face which was . . . wrong. The eyes were bright and alert, but no hint of recognition came to the surrounding features. The whole face was a parody.

His heart lurched towards despair. He had been so sure his guesses were correct! But now, as Dan rose and began to make towards him, seeming puzzled, he was poised to turn and flee. The Dan Sakky he knew would have exclaimed with pleasure at seeing an old friend, come to clap him on the back and ask how he had been. Whereas this creature—

"It's all right, Dennis," a soft voice said at his side, and he started. Unnoticed, Parvati had crept up. She too was unclothed, but over her shoulder she had a sort of crude basket on a sling, woven from supple plant-stems, in which she had placed a dozen assorted samples of Asgard vegetation. "That's the price which has to be paid. Though if you worked out enough of the truth to bring you here looking for us, I don't suppose I need to tell you that."

She put her hand out, and Dan took it obediently. He sat down on his heels again and stared curiously at Dennis.

Tearing his attention away, Dennis rounded on Parvati. She at least was sane and in good health, and he wanted to fall on her shoulder and weep away the dreadful anxiety of the past few weeks. But all he could manage to do was say—as it seemed to him, inanely— "I thought I saw you just now. On the base island."

She smiled and linked her fingers with his. "It's weird, isn't it?" she said. "I mean the way one's subconscious keeps sending up messages, and they come through to awareness in the most extraordinary forms . . . Oh, *Dennis!*"

She snatched away the hand that Dan was holding and abruptly flung her arms about his neck. Then there was a time when all he knew was a series of frantic kisses and the touch of her smooth tear-wet face on his stubbly cheek, and vaguely, at the edge of perception, Dan wandering off to inspect another nearby plant, grimacing at them occasionally.

Finally he was able to whisper, close to her ear, "You are really all right, then—all of you?"

"Of course. More or less. I mean, we're all still alive and well, and we've managed to fix up shelters and we're gradually working out what's useful and what isn't. That's the reason for this basket I'm carrying, of course. And for the state Dan's in. It's his turn."

A blinding light broke in on Dennis's mind. He stepped back from Parvati and pointed a shaky finger at Dan. He repeated, "His turn? You mean it's deliberate?"

"It's the only way, Dennis," Parvati said soberly. "You must realise that—don't you?"

Dennis closed his eyes briefly, recalling a period of ten days lost from his life when he had apparently behaved just as Dan was doing now: wandering about the diamond island at the beck and call of instinct, sleeping where he grew tired, sampling the vegetation and digesting it or bring it up again.

"I—ah—I got poisoned, I think," he said at last. "I went swimming and crossed the path of something which I guess must be like a stinging jellyfish. And then there were ten days when I don't remember anything which makes sense. Yet I'm the only person, over there on the base island, who isn't fit to drop from scurvy. That's it, isn't it?"

Parvati looked horrified. "You must have had a terrible time!" she exclaimed. "It must have been violent! Ours was gentle, at least, even though it was alarming before we realised what it was doing to us."

"What *is* it doing?" Dennis demanded. "I think if someone doesn't make it clear to me soon, I'll start screaming."

"Did you ever keep a dog?" she said after a moment for thought. "Did you ever see one drag itself across country when it was so sick it could barely stand, in search of a special kind of grass which would make its belly reject the poison it had swallowed? We've got to be our own dogs, as it were. Our bodies know things which our minds never can. So what we have to do is turn our minds off, and bit by bit we're figuring out how."

Dennis stared in dismay at Dan, who had now located a sort of fungus growing on the side of a wood-plant, and was testing a flake of it with a critical expression. Shortly he spat it out and moved on.

"But if one has to go insane in order to stay alive—" he began, and Parvati cut him short.

"No, Dennis! That's the whole point! Don't think of what's happening to Dan, or what happened to you, as 'going insane'. It's the exact opposite! You went *sane*—totally and completely sane!"

EIGHT   BEYOND THE WIDE WORLD'S END

With an host of furious fancies
Whereof I am commander
With a burning spear, and a horse of air,
To the wilderness I wander.
By a knight of ghosts and shadows
I summoned am to tourney
Ten leagues beyond the wide world's end—
Methinks it is no journey.
   All while I sing, "Any food, any feeding,
   Money, drink or clothing?
   Come dame or maid, be not afraid—
   Poor Tom will injure nothing."
                —Tom o' Bedlam's Song

XXII

HOPELESSLY BAFFLED BY the paradox Parvati had offered him, Dennis stared at her blankly. She gave an impatient shrug and settled her basket more easily on its sling.

"It's not much good my talking to you on my own," she said. "You need Tai's theory, and Abdul's, as well as mine, before it'll come clear. I'll take you to them now. Dan's almost due to fall asleep, I guess, and I have five or six things in the bag which we haven't collected before."

"You mean he—?" Dennis nodded at Dan.

"Yes, of course. What do you think we're doing? Each of us in turn is acting like a—what's the term Ulla dredged up? Ah yes!—a truffle-hound. Before they found out how to cultivate truffles commercially, they used to rely on trained dogs or pigs which snuffed them out. We only have ourselves, as I said. So we're selecting a number of native plants by instinct, which we can later evaluate consciously. We've found a substance we can chew for a bit which does what this poisonous fish did to you—temporarily suspend the higher levels of the mind—and today Dan's been dosing himself, and I've been taking samples of anything he approved of."

"You—turn your mind off?" Dennis said in dismay, thinking of the shock he would have had if he had encountered Parvati, rather than Dan, in that condition.

"It was my turn yesterday," she said matter-of-factly. "That's why I'm on basket duty. Tomorrow Dan will go out with Kitty. But come along—let's not stand around. You too, Dan!"

Compliant as a well-trained dog, Dan fell in behind them as she turned to lead the way.

There was nothing of modern Earth—that sophisticated, domesticated planet—about the settlement to which she brought him. There were no level plane roofs, no meticulously machined planks. Yet there was incontestably something of mankind about it, for all that it was composed of lean-to structures against a convenient rock wall, made of boughs and sheets of bark plastered over with natural mud and left to dry.

Crude they might be, but these peculiar little sheds were unique. No creatures on Asgard except humans built anything on land.

Surrounding the "hamlet," in which the centrepiece was formed by a large stone hearth piled with ashes, there were patches of cultivated ground, and he recognised established plants of spinach, beans, potatoes, corn, a dozen or more varieties. Each plant was surrounded by a tiny moat into which raw sewage had been poured, judging by the smell. Tai and Kitty were tending them; Abdul was adding a new layer of adobe to one of the walls, and Ulla was doing something with the fibrous stalks of a native plant which rang a chord of memory in Dennis's mind. As a child he had seen in a history-book a picture of the way in which flax used to be gathered and allowed to rot before the long strands that became linen could be teased out.

Some problems have the same solution no matter where you are. But others . . .

At sight of him they dropped their tasks and came running. There was hand-shaking, and clapping on shoulders, and a frantic kiss from Kitty which went on so long it proved that one characteristic of the little Greek meteorologist had survived the astonishing change all these people had undergone. Finally he had a chance to look them over, and was instantly struck by a crucial truth.

Deprived of all the aids which had been brought from Earth to make colonisation of Asgard easy, they had managed to preserve the single indispensable advantage which the people on the well-equipped base island had lost.

They were all healthy.

Underfed to the point of gauntness—Abdul was positively stringy now, and even Tai's blocky body had hardened down to its essential muscle, innocent of fat—they yet exuded vitality, and were so eager to discuss what they had learned with an outsider that Abdul had to reassert his former chairmanship and call them to order.

They sat down—crosslegged on the ground, because furniture was still in the luxury stage as far as this Asgard subculture was concerned—except for Dan, who lay down against the rock wall where they had sited their lean-tos, and shortly began to snore quietly. Dennis kept uneasily eyeing him while Parvati went to a natural hollow in the rock which was serving as a dish and dipped from it cupfuls of a dark liquid which she offered around.

"We're calling this tea," she explained to Dennis. "It's an infusion of sun-dried vegetable cuttings. You may not like it, but it does something which feels right. Try it."

Dubiously he accepted his cup, and Abdul said dryly, "At least the tradition of hospitality towards strangers is off to a good start on this planet. How does it strike you?"

Dennis shrugged, unable to tell if he liked or disliked the brew. But, like the bit of bark he had chewed earlier, it seemed to assuage an unfamiliar lack. The speed of events had left him behind, though, and he felt dazed.

Sensing his difficulty, Parvati filled a short gap by telling the others about the poisonous creature he had run foul of, and his ten lost days.

"You remember something from the period in question, though?" Abdul suggested.

Dennis licked his lips. "Uh—yes. But the memories don't fit what I know very well I did!"

"I think you're probably wrong," Abdul countered. "Suppose you tell us what you do remember, in the greatest possible detail."

Frowning, Dennis complied as best he could. Until now, prompted by the obvious interest of his companions, he had dismissed all this as dream-stuff, the product of delirium. As he struggled to organise his impressions, however, he realised they differed from dreams, which fade with time. These images were if anything fresher than at first. Detail he might not have related the following day accrued to his recital until he had elaborated a long, complex and astonishing coherent story. There was a hero, and there was an island across the western sea, and there was a journey to it, and there were calamities . . .

Before he had ended it, his listeners were jogging up and down with glee they could barely control. The moment he finished, Kitty burst out, "But that's perfect! It's exactly what you said, Parvati—isn't it?"

"Stop the doubletalk!" Dennis almost shouted. "Tell me what's happened to me!"

"Well, if I understand Parvati's reasoning," Abdul said, "you've lived a legend. And so have we. For the first time in human history, the people whose experiences will later become the myths and legends which shape the subsequent culture have known what they were doing when they did it. Thanks to the planners who stocked our minds with images from Earthly tradition before sending us here to fend for ourselves, we have the necessary insights to appreciate our experiences both as individuals and as—well, as demigods."

Dazed, Dennis shook his head uncomprehendingly.

"Think of it this way," Parvati said. "Back on Earth, in almost every country, there were real events which became transmuted into legends, which magnify historical facts to supernatural proportions, and myths, which use fact as a basis to symbolise continuing truths of human existence like birth and death. Indian tradition glorifies the conquering Aryans, who came with horses and chariots and a divine intoxicant called 'soma'. Irish tradition dwells wistfully on the former proud independent peoples who were driven to the west by better-armed barbarians, and vanished. Now what we've done is—is the stuff of epics, isn't it?"

"You can say that again," Ulla murmured. "My Viking ancestors never did anything comparable. Even the Vinland settlers died out. And if they'd survived the most they could have done was exploit a new continent. We're unique, Dennis, and we don't have to be modest about it. We're the only people who tore the whole damned planet out from under our feet and put another one in place of it!"

"And your subconscious knows this," Parvati said. "That's what it's been trying to tell you, in the only language it has available. The island which lay on the sea and looked like the moon—consider that in relation to your obsession with Asgard's moon, where Pyotr died. And don't imagine you hid from *me* the jealousy you felt because you wished you had died in his place! Equation: moon equals Land of the Blest equals Asgard, the favoured paradise in the sky to which the hero makes his voyage."

Kitty, seeing the expression that was spreading over Dennis's face, chuckled. "I think the man is catching on!"

"Yes!" Excited, Dennis leaned forward. "That fits the *geasa*, too. I must have felt I was cursed by being stranded here. And the magic cauldron I lost by flinging it at the moon in a fit of temper—that's the *Pinta*, with equipment on board which could have made life safe for us here."

"And so on," Parvati nodded. "And that's what the people on the base island haven't yet learned. Their bodies are on Asgard, and their bodies know that. But their minds are still half on Earth. Eventually simple hunger may drive them to face the facts, but there's a dreadful risk they may be too weak from starvation by then to benefit from what their instincts can tell them."

"That's more or less what I've been feeling lately," Dennis said, frowning. "I seem to have been looking at the potential of Asgard for its own sake, so I've been getting things done. But the rest of them seem to be looking at the ways it fails to measure up to Earth."

"Yes, the transition is horribly difficult," nodded Abdul. "It's a shock to the vanity, if nothing else, to realise that Asgard-Man isn't master of his planet, a member of a multi-billion society which can afford to rack up knowledge on dusty shelves on the vague chance that someone may one day find it useful for a doctorate thesis. He's a species competing from scratch with others who got here first, and he's got to behave as such, or he'll become extinct.

"On the other hand, of course, when I compared us to demigods I wasn't joking. If we do win out, when our descendants look back generations from now, they will recognise that we, and we only, are the ones who made the big jump across the lightyears. Did Parvati tell you what must have happened when you got poisoned by that stinging fish?"

"She said," Dennis answered slowly, "that it drove me sane."

"That's right. We tend to think of sanity as being what other people find acceptable. But what account do animals take of public opinion? No, what sanity consists in is doing what *the planet you live on* will accept. And precisely because Asgard is not Earth, what is sane here may well seem crazy in Earthly terms.

"So what we have to do—what we've desperately been trying to find a way of doing—is drive the entire Asgard colony Asgard-sane."

XXIII

THERE WAS A pause. Eventually Dennis said, "Was it—uh—'Asgard-sane' to sabotage all that equipment, or was it done in a fit of blind fury?"

"It was the best we could manage," Parvati said. "And it didn't work. You see, when we'd had a chance to talk together about the various experiences we'd had, mentally, we realised the fatal flaw in our existing plan. It's impossible to do what we were trying to do—conquer Asgard wholly by the power of reason. Man isn't a rational being. He's a rational *animal*, and unless the animal and human parts of us are perfectly integrated we shall always live here as strangers. Which would be absurd—this is an incredibly hospitable world for human beings! But when we tried to explain what we'd figured out to people like Saul and Tibor, we found them so attached to the rational approach they wouldn't listen. They were even proposing to lock us up at gunpoint because we wanted to do things which didn't fit their logical attitude: drink unpurified water, eat native-grown plants, and sweat out the necessary period of transition to an Asgard diet."

"When I found myself absent-mindedly chewing on a bit of woodplant bark, I thought for a moment I was crazy," Dennis said. "If I hadn't had the evidence of my survival on the diamond island, I'd have rushed straight for a medical check."

"Of course." That was Tai speaking up. The blocky Chinese hunched forward, his face very serious. "Any of us would have felt the same if we hadn't been—ah—taken by surprise. Look, let me explain what goes on when you try and adapt to an Asgard diet, shall I? It's complicated, but the essential factor is this. Your body is wiser than your mind; it's been around longer, and carries memories in its cells which we've barely begun to guess at."

"I gave him your image of a dog looking for emetic grasses," Parvati said.

"And I'd already thought of something related to that," Dennis said, and quoted the example of the pioneer submariners.

"That shows insight," Tai approved. "But there's another point. Know anything about sheep-farming? No? Well, there's an important Earthly grazing grass called *Phalaris tuberosa* which sheep normally eat quite happily. Sometimes, though, when they browse off young spring shoots, they get a disease called staggers from it. That's due to an unusual concentration of tryptamine alkaloids. What was harmless yesterday suddenly exceeds the tolerance level, and—" Tai snapped his fingers. "Now our tolerance level is much lower than that of a sheep because our nervous system is more complex. Plants like the opium poppy, or the coca plant, can hit us with so damned many permutations of alkaloids it took advanced computers to sort them out, and some of them affect us in such minuscule concentrations you'd need a Shlovsky-Har fractionator to detect them. We lost ours. That was why, when I called for test subjects, I knew I was taking a risk. And the risk proved to exist, although luckily . . ." He hesitated, scowling into nowhere.

"You know what a vitamin precursor is?"

"A substance which the body can metabolise into the vitamin form," Dennis said promptly.

"Correct. Well, what we ingest from Asgard vegetation, whether it's of Earthly or indigenous stock, includes a hallucinogen precursor. And—ho, brother!" Tai chuckled ruefully. "Lysergic acid is weak compared to *this* stuff! I think what we do is hang a urea group on the molecule, which our test animals couldn't because they aren't primates, and I also suspect that it blocks amine oxidase more efficiently than anything we ever dreamed up on Earth, thus shooting the serotonin balance to hell. But that's irrelevant. What counts is this. What does a hallucinogen do?"

"It destroys perceptual sets, isn't that right?"

"That's the standard definition," Parvati said. "But did you ever stop to think *exactly* what that statement means? 'Except ye become as little children . . .'!"

Drawn as though by a magnet, Dennis's gaze fixed on the sleeping form of Dan Sakky.

"That's right," Abdul confirmed. "We've found a way to strip ourselves of all sophistication. We can approach what grows on Asgard with an animal lack of inhibition, and let our cellular memory judge what's safe and what isn't." He shivered, as though in awe. "It's almost as though the entire trend of human culture was towards the colonisation of other worlds! That's what gives me my confidence in our ultimate success. Something's been working like a leaven in human thinking, preparing us psychologically for the process of dying and being reborn as a different species. Asgard-Man is only the first of many, I'm certain."

"What happens when you take this—this drug you've discovered?" Dennis said after a pause.

"The conscious mind is suspended," Parvati said. "Just as happened to you on the diamond island. It shunts a human being from an Earthly into an Asgard frame of reference."

"A species which isn't hampered by thinking about what it's doing, but responding to what its belly and glands tell it, has the edge on an alien world." Looking pleased with his summation, Tai leaned back against the nearby rock wall.

"But one gets over it?" Dennis demanded.

"No, it's cumulative," Parvati said. "That's why it took two or three days for the stuff to work the first time on us six."

"But you're communicating with me now okay," Dennis said.

"Ah, I see what you mean. You take the stuff, it begins to work, and then for six to eight hours you behave like an animal, retaining only species-recognition and certain other traits we regard as human. Eventually you fall asleep, as Dan's doing right now, and this gives the brain a chance to absorb and file the alien images acquired during the experience. You do know, presumably, that the only purpose of going to sleep is to get some dreaming done? The human body is far too efficient to need so much inactivity, but the brain isn't."

"Y-yes." Dennis was frowning with concentration.

"And, during the sleep, the mind organises the impressions it's stored into the most acceptable form it can. Your own images drawn from Irish legend are an example. Eventually—at least this is what we're hoping—we'll get rid of all our Earthly preconceptions:

this food is good, that is bad, this place is safe, that's dangerous. And we'll have acquired Asgard replacements for them, which will allow us to relax and be happy here."

Parvati leaned forward. "Haven't you noticed that ever since we arrived the only thing which has made the colonists happy is feeling that we're making this planet over in the image of Earth? We couldn't *ever* do that! We've been chasing a ghost!"

"I suppose we have," Dennis admitted. "And this is what you were trying to drive them to face when you—ah—sabotaged everything?"

"We couldn't make them understand that it was essential to do the same as we'd done," Abdul said. "Their minds simply closed up, *snap!* All they could see was that one morning we'd been found babbling about gods and demons, and they wouldn't admit we could have learned anything from the experience. So on the spur of the moment we thought we'd call in the help of hunger and thirst—smash the dam, put native-grown food in with the supplies, wipe the computer memories to throw them back on what their bodies could tell them . . ." He sighed. "It didn't work. It made them more hostile than ever."

"Damned right it did," Dennis muttered. He hesitated for a moment. "You know, the more I think about this, the more sense it makes! Everything fits—even the *sid*."

"What?" Kitty said.

"The *sid* in my vision. The fairyland where one night can be a hundred years. It's a metaphor for the timelessness of qua-space, obviously." Dennis's voice rose in excitement. "And there's something else, too! I suddenly remembered that I was wondering when I set off on my trip to hunt for diamonds whether our skills were too great for what we were trying to do."

"I'm not surprised," Parvati said. "You were the only outsider among us, the only unwilling colonist. You've always had detachment the rest of us couldn't match." She gave him a warm smile and laid her hand briefly on his. "What's more, of course, you'd already been overtaken by what you called a trap that Asgard sprung on you."

Dennis nodded, thinking of his fit of madness with Sigrid, which had amazingly done him no harm. "How did the truth come to you, then? How did your subconscious interpret it into terms you could understand and act upon?"

"As I told you," Abdul said, "this is the first time the protagonists of legends have been able to appreciate them on both levels. All our visions had two things in common. First, they drew images from our own particular traditions, and second, they stressed real-life preoccupations—the moon, where so many of our companions died, the food problem, owing to the outbreak of scurvy, and so on. I saw myself being made to eat the bread and drink the water offered by Ament, the ancient Egyptian goddess who was called 'The Lady of the West'. And that ties in interestingly with your image of sailing westward beyond the sunset, doesn't it?" He shook his head wonderingly. "Presumably we've always thought of the night sky in which stars appear as lying to the west . . . Never mind that for the moment, though. What this was supposed to do was to make you a 'friend of the gods'; in other words, you had to enter the Hall of Double Justice where men's souls are judged, and once in the other world you could never return to Earth."

A shiver of awe went down Dennis's spine.

"It bears out what the poet Graves used to teach, back in the twentieth century," Parvati said. "He maintained there were two kinds of truth, scientific and poetic. He called them Apollonian and Dionysian. We've learned a poetic truth. The same sort of thing happened to me. I hammered together images from half a dozen different branches of Indian mythology and they wound up making sense. The moon in some stories is regarded as the abode of the dead, the kingdom of Yama who was the first man ever to die. But in others it's the reservoir of the divine intoxicant 'soma', which the gods regularly drain—hence the phases of the moon, you see? When I came to myself, I found I was identifying my breasts, as sources of milk, with the waning moon as a source of soma, and covering one of them up because it seemed wrong for there to be two!"

"I had the moon and the food problem in my visions, too," Tai Men said. "I was obsessed with the ancient ceremony of making offerings to the moon, which only women took part in because the patron being of the moon—the Hare—is also regarded as the patron of inverts. I think my subconscious was saying a very Chinese thing to me: that if I wanted descendants to do honour to my memory, I must stop paying attention to the moon. In other words, I must stop being afraid of dying under an alien sun, as the crew of the *Pinta* did, and face the truth of my own mortality."

"That's akin to what I remember!" Dennis exclaimed. "I—uh—I *woke up* realising that even the great heroes must die."

"Most of us seem to have been concerned about that," Abdul said. "Dan told us about his visions, and they all centred on the ancient tribal secret societies of his ancestors, the initiates who passed on tribal lore from generation to generation, and inspired themselves by inhaling the smoke of sacred herbs—read 'eating local plants for the sake of the visions they induce', if you like. He was concerned about the moon, too. He recounted a story about how people tried to build a tower and climb to it, to discover what it was. The tower fell down, and most of them were killed. But the idea of death wasn't depressing, as he explained it. The spirits of the ancestors who died so that their descendants could live in prosperity were a simple fact of life, not something you could resent."

He glanced across at the Negro. "Parvati, I think he's waking up—will you take care of him?"

Nodding, Parvati rose and went over to him. Dennis heard her murmuring in a soothing tone as Kitty Minakis took up the tale.

"I saw the base island as the afterworld," she said. "The place where the sun never shines—and let's face it, Old Sol doesn't shine here except as a star, does it? —surrounded by the rivers you have to buy passage across. And one of them, of course, is Lethe, whose waters you drink to forget about Earth."

"That was lucky," Ulla said wryly. "I'm sure it was your obsession with Charon's ferry which led you to make off with that cushionfoil! It was the one which had been stocked up for three people to go in search of you," she amplified for Dennis's benefit. "We've got it hidden in the bushes yonder. When you turned us loose from the cage Saul shut us up in, she came and fetched us off the base island, and the supplies on board kept us going while we made our night-time raids and fetched the seeds and what was left of the gibberellins which made our little garden possible. Not that we have to depend exclusively on Earthly crops, of course—not now. It was you, wasn't it, who stopped the overnight watch in the *Santa Maria*?"

Dennis nodded.

"We owe you a lot, then. We were terrified when we sneaked in and stole the growth-accelerators!"

"Nobody told me any had disappeared!" Dennis said, startled.

"They were probably too confused," Ulla shrugged. "Thought Tai had poured them down the drain with everything else."

"Maybe." Dennis sighed. "What visions did you have, by the way?"

"Oh, in the best pessimistic tradition of my ancestors I was obsessed with the resurrection motifs from the story of Odin. The message of those is that it doesn't matter what you do—embalm the head of all-wise Mimir, i.e. draw on the knowledge in the ship's computers, or drink Kvasir's blood and become a skald, i.e. eat the local vegetation—you still wind up dead. It wasn't till I had a chance to compare what I'd undergone with what my subconscious was saying. You see, after the *Ragnar rökkr,* the Twilight of the Gods, there's a new creation. And—well, goodness, isn't this very planet named after the land beyond Bifrost, the rainbow bridge?"

A great calm was settling on Dennis's tormented mind. He said, "So what is it we must do? There are all those people on the base island, and— Well, I've been watching them the past few weeks, and I can say for sure we can't rely on them responding to what their bellies tell them to do. They're sick with scurvy, they're aware of what it is and what it does, and they must have noticed that while you were shut up in the cage for them to gawp at you remained in reasonable health. Hell, they've been hounded and chivvied by me, and I'm certainly not ill and apathetic! Yet in spite of the evidence of their own eyes they're drifting along in the same rigid pattern as before."

"They're colonising Asgard from the head instead of the guts, then!"

The call came from Dan Sakky, sitting up with Parvati's help, his back against the rock wall. "Hello, Dennis," he added, knuckling sleep from his eyes and fighting a yawn. "Good to see you over here. Parvati says you reached the same conclusions we did, only you took a rather more drastic route." He lost the battle with the yawn, and the words died in an enormous sigh.

Astonished, but relieved, at the rapidity with which Dan had recovered from his self-induced mindlessness, Dennis returned his greeting and reverted to the problem he had just voiced.

"Look, even if we manage to do something like— well, sneaking into the mess-hall by night and pouring native-grown foodstuffs into the supplies—what's going to become of all those people?"

"They're going to do exactly what mankind has done throughout history," Dan said. He got awkwardly to his feet and hobbled over to take his place in the circle, moving stiffly as though he had become cramped during his deep slumber. "They're going to become ghosts so that their children's children may till fertile fields and raise their families in peace."

Ghosts? Was this something from the vision Dan's subconscious had generated during the period he was under the drug? Dennis looked inquiringly at Abdul, and discovered that the latter seemed to have made perfect sense of the remark.

"That's right," he said. "They're going to measure the seasonal rise and fall of rivers, and be judged according to whether they replaced the boundary marks honestly, or moved them in their own favour through misuse of superior knowledge."

"They are going to acquire great wisdom," Ulla said. "And still they will die. It's the lot of us all."

"They are going to work and save and struggle," Kitty said, "and at the end all they will carry out of the world will be the fare to pay their passage into the land of the dead."

"They will call themselves to account by the measure of us their ancestors," Tai Men said. "They will judge themselves as to wisdom and mercy and justice by what we, here, now, decide is wise and merciful and just."

His face was suddenly downcast, as though he had heard his own words in memory and realised what a burden he had taken on himself.

"The mother of all, who is Kali," Parvati said, "went mad and slew her man. But that too was divine, the anger which drove her. There is the Creator, there is the Preserver, there is the Destroyer. All three are one, and the time of destruction is upon us." There was a dreadful authority in her voice which Dennis had never expected to hear from any living being: the authority which dictated the fate of worlds. "We must go over there to break and burn. We must poison their food and steep bruised stems in their water. And what will happen then will be very terrible."

"It's the end of summer," Abdul said greyly. "There will be gales, high tides, storms. Perhaps some will not listen to what hunger and thirst tell them. Perhaps they will have to be overpowered. But this is a hard universe, and if there is a law, I suppose it says: 'Thou shalt live!' "

Parvati put her hands to her forehead for a moment, as though giddy, and Dennis wondered if an instant of divine insight had come and gone. Then, suddenly, she smiled quite normally and put her hand out to close it over his.

"We'll obey that law," she said. "Given the chance, so will our friends. And so will our children—won't they?"

"Tonight?" Dennis said. He meant two things by the question, and the woman meant two things by the answering nod she gave.

* * *

So, secretly under cover of dark, they went out—the seven of them—and loosed the bonds of Earth from all the folk. Before dawn the seed of a new species had been planted, which would be master of the planet.

And the name of that species also was Man.

XXIV

EXCERPT FROM APPENDIX *to summary version of official* Findings, *Third Manned Expedition to Sigma Draconis*:

"In spite of its obvious resemblance to the sacred writings of various ancient Earthly cultures, the foregoing text is in no way regarded by the inhabitants of 'Asgard' as constituting a myth or legend. No element of the supernatural attaches to the marvellous events therein recorded, any more than was accorded by the natives to our own arrival. Just as, although the accomplishment of qua-space travel is currently beyond their abilities, they take its feasibility on trust (and not as a matter of faith, but as being consonant with what they have learned for themselves about the nature of the universe), so they accept that the semi-divine characters of this pseudo-historical record—Great Mother Parvati, Kitty the sister of the winter storm, and the rest—were in fact human beings like themselves only operating on a different perceptual basis.

"Indeed, careful comparison of the surviving records of the Second Expedition with the version of the story given above (which was collated from written and oral versions current on all 736 populated islands on the planet) suggests that there were real personages corresponding to every one of the named characters, although the rôles allotted are not always as logically assigned as in the case of 'Kitty, sister of the winter storm.' This would presumable have been Kitty Minakis, the meteorologist.

"Precisely how Parvati—if this is Parvati Chandra, as one might expect—acquired the epithet of 'Great Mother' is still debatable, however, as is the remarkable transformation of the character presumed to be the counterpart of the historical Dennis Malone into a kind of fusion of Odin, Osiris, Attis, Jesus and all the other resurrection-symbols of Earthly mythology. That some such equation is intended cannot be contested; he is the spouse of the Great Mother, the father of the first child to be born alive on Asgard, and the patron ancestor of the quasi-guild (see *Division of Labour*) responsible for opening up new islands for habitation. Indeed the current head of this guild claims direct descent from him in the male line.

"And he, like all his contemporaries, takes it for granted both that 'Dennis' was a man like himself, and that he died and rose again. Furthermore, he maintains that this altruistic saviour committed premeditated mass murder by poisoning one hundred and seventy-four (the figure is invariable and hence probably literal) of his companions, stealthily by night, with the aid of what Staff Psychologist Nefre-Bell has astutely termed his 'disciples', although as Staff Psychologist Jensen-Juarez points out they have many of the attributes of a pantheon rather than a group of mortals.

"As a consequence of this poisoning, the others went holily insane (see Section *IX* of the narrative, above). We are tentatively inclined to the view that this extremely dramatic passage enshrines memories of a real event, possibly the discovery that certain Asgard plants can be digested by human beings after a period of acclimatisation, and that some process analogous to the deification or sanctification of men who brought useful arts (e.g. writing) to primitive cultures on Earth is operating here. Nefre-Bell has nicknamed it the 'Prometheus' syndrome, but not all the staff psychologists go along with his view that the motivating force behind it is the rescue of the colony from an otherwise certain doom.

"Indeed, it is impossible to see from what doom the colony might have needed to be rescued! Setting apart the loss of one of the three ships—believed from examination of the wreckage embedded in the surface of the moon to have been the *Pinta*—and the catastrophes immediately following the landing which resulted in such lesser setbacks as the wiping of most of the computer memories and the outbreak of a serious fire owing to faults in the cooking equipment, which seems to have destroyed several of the first buildings to be erected on the base island, the colony's progress appears to have been astonishing and continuous.

"It was only to be expected that the transfer of humanity from its home planet to another, foreign world would result in a kind of culture-shock. Accordingly it is of small importance to find that at present we are baffled by the mixture of hard historical truth and near-legendary exaggeration which we find in such stories as the foregoing. The language may look familiar, but we should bear in mind that it is being employed by people whose life-experience differs totally from our own on Earth. This is a point well appreciated by the people of Asgard themselves, who—when we expressed out inability to grasp the subtler referents compressed into a particular phrase—declared cheerfully that from our point of view they were all completely insane, so they'd expected us to have trouble! (This, incidentally, is something they claim to have been taught by the Great Mother Parvati and her spouse Dennis.)

"Nefre-Bell has suggested that what we found on Asgard is a human culture which begins where our own leaves off—in other words, that the highly elaborate and sophisticated traditions of Earth constitute for the inhabitants of that planet only the base-line from which they will advance in a new direction we can barely guess at. This is a fascinating and tantalising concept, but as Jensen-Juarez justifiably points out it will require far more exhaustive investigation than we were able to give it during our brief stay of one quarter-year.

"In any case, though, the foregoing narrative is proof in itself that the brave pioneers who are now long dead on an alien planet left behind them a branch of mankind both sufficiently endowed with animal vigour to establish themselves in face of competition from species whose native world they had trespassed upon, and— what may after all be far more important—sufficiently human to create within a few generations their own indigenous myths, legends, epics, traditions: in sum, everything which constitutes 'a culture' in the ordinary sense. We may look forward . . ."

ABOUT THE AUTHOR

John Brunner was born in England in 1934 and educated at Cheltenham College. He sold his first novel in 1951 and has been publishing sf steadily since then. His books have won him international acclaim from both mainstream and genre audiences. His most famous novel, the classic *Stand on Zanzibar*, won the Hugo Award for Best Novel in 1969, the British Science Fiction Award, and the Prix Apollo in France. Mr. Brunner lives in Somerset, England.